COAL BOY

A Novel

GUERNICA WORLD EDITIONS 59

COAL BOY

A Novel

ALBAN KOJIMA

TORONTO—CHICAGO—BUFFALO—LANCASTER (U.K.)
2023

Guernica Editions Founder: Antonio D'Alfonso

Michael Mirolla, editor
Cover design: Allen Jomoc Jr.
Interior design: Jill Ronsley, suneditwrite.com

Guernica Editions Inc.
287 Templemead Drive, Hamilton (ON), Canada L8W 2W4
2250 Military Road, Tonawanda, N.Y. 14150-6000 U.S.A.
www.guernicaeditions.com

Distributors:
Independent Publishers Group (IPG)
600 North Pulaski Road, Chicago IL 60624
University of Toronto Press Distribution (UTP)
5201 Dufferin Street, Toronto (ON), Canada M3H 5T8
Gazelle Book Services, White Cross Mills
High Town, Lancaster LA1 4XS U.K.

First edition.

Legal Deposit—First Quarter
Library of Congress Catalog Card Number: 2022943576
Library and Archives Canada Cataloguing in Publication
Title: Coal boy : a novel / Alban Kojima.
Names: Kojima, Alban, author.
Series: Guernica world editions ; 59.
Description: Series statement: Guernica world editions ; 59
Identifiers: Canadiana (print) 20220398313 | Canadiana (ebook) 20220398321 | ISBN 9781771837910 (softcover) | ISBN 9781771837927 (EPUB)
Classification: LCC PS3611.O485 C63 2023 | DDC 813/.6—dc23

PART 01

Mitsukaidō

1958 ~ 1959

October 1958

"I HEAR MRS. Kon and the children," Nao said to no one in particular. She kept washing rice bowls and chopsticks in the bucket of water she had brought in late the previous night from the well outside the kitchen.

The sliding closet door by the alcove in the six-*tatami* room slammed shut.

In the closet, Uruo pushed stacks of *futon* and blankets further back against the wall so that he could curl up in the corner where his grandmother, Nao, could not reach him. The smell of the *futon* and the pungent scent of the old wooden shelf that spread above his head and divided the closet into two levels assuring Uruo that he was safe. He leaned against a *futon* stack, with its soft fabric on the side of his face. He closed his eyes.

Uruo heard his own heartbeat. The dark silence brought forth the faces of children in his first-grade class at school who, pointing their fingers at him, whispered to each other: "That's the coal boy." Uruo had heard another name uttered at him recently: "Black Buddha." Because he had curly black hair like Buddha. The children who were now with Mrs. Kon, waiting for him to join them, might not be the same ones who called him "coal boy" or "Buddha"; but they were not his friends either. Every morning when they stopped by his house, they clustered about Mrs. Kon as if to keep away from him. And, often, when Mrs. Kon extended her hand to take Uruo's hand, one of the children would slip in between Mrs. Kon and Uruo to grasp her hand first, as if to protect her from this dark, strange creature in front of them.

⁓

Later that night, while soaking in the wooden bathtub with Nao, Uruo asked: "Why do they call me 'coal boy' and 'Buddha'?"

"Your name is Uruo. Tell them you're Uruo Yusa." Nao looked into Uruo's hazel eyes.

"We use coals in *hibachi* in winter, don't we?"

"Yes. They burn red and warm up our house. That's a good thing."

"A Buddha sits in our family altar, too."

"And his hair is curly like yours, haven't you noticed it? Those small ringlets on his head? They tell us how deep and immense His wisdom is. He is the holiest of all, child." In the warm water scented by the floating iris petals, Nao touched Uruo's back, drew his little body closer to hers, and held him in her arms for a long time.

"Is my hair like Buddha's, Grandma?"

"Yours is softer and looser than his, like gentle waves in the ocean." Holding Uruo in one arm, Nao gently stroked his wet hair with the other hand, smiling at how it bounced right back to its curls.

Uruo clung to her.

⁓

Uruo wished Mrs. Kon and the children would go away. He wanted the stillness in the closet to last forever. But he knew his wish would not come true: the closet door was already sliding open. He covered his eyes with the palm of his hand. Then Nao's face peeked into the darkness, gazing at him and whispering: "Come out, son. It's all right."

Uruo covered his face with a blanket and retreated farther into the *futon* stack.

"Mrs. Kon loves you. Don't you know that? She wants to hold your hand and walk you to the school."

Nothing mattered to him. He only wanted to stay in the closet.

"You are coming out, aren't you?"

Uruo remained silent until he saw the door had slid shut.

"Uruo." Mrs. Kon's faint voice, sounding like a mosquito buzzing, flew by once.

All turned quiet.

He had no idea how long he had slept in the closet. Uruo panicked at the thought that he might have gone blind. Then he remembered he had put a blanket over his face before he fell asleep.

He pulled the blanket off.

Still, the darkness blocked his sight.

He pushed the *futon* stack away and crawled forward, feeling for the door pull. His fingertip found a small round dent on the upper left of the door and he slid the door open.

The *tatami* floor no longer reflected the sunlight. They were worn out and colorless. Outside, in the hencoop, the chickens were cackling.

He got up and walked out to the veranda that encircled the east and south sides of the six-*tatami* room. He slipped on a pair of straw sandals three times larger than his feet and was about to saunter out to the backyard when a loud creaking coming from the small room above the hencoop stopped him.

"Aunt Kureo?" Uruo whispered.

His aunt Kureo Doi and her son Hanbo had never visited Nao's house in the town of Mitsukaidō. Then, two years ago, in 1956, when Uruo was four years old, they suddenly showed up. Hanbo wore a wrinkled white short-sleeved shirt and a pair of faded black pants with their knees patched. He was holding two loads of things in wrapping cloths in his hands and carried a large wicker suitcase strapped around his shoulders. Kureo had a small wicker suitcase on her back and two bulging wrapping cloths in her hands. They brought in a moldy odor with them, perhaps emanating from their wicker suitcases.

Uruo had never forgotten Kureo's face when she first saw him peeking at them from behind Nao. Kureo recoiled. She furrowed, her eyes radiating a fierce beam as cold as ice that could pierce Uruo's forehead.

"Aoi's son," Nao said. "I know what you're thinking, Kureo. You lost your husband in Iwo Jima. I don't blame you." She paused. Looking directly at Kureo, Nao continued: "Uruo is a good boy."

Kureo's right fingers touched the sliding front door behind her.

"Don't!" Nao said. "You don't have the money to go back to Kagoshima, anyway. Or do you?"

"You shouldn't be doing that." Kureo hissed at her son who was already playing a game of peekaboo with Uruo.

"He's my little cousin, Mom." Hanbo casually sat down on the threshold that led into the eight-*tatami* room and began unloading his wicker suitcase.

"I'm Hanbo. Come here, little one." Smiling, Uruo's sixteen-year-old cousin extended his arms.

"Uruo." Nao turned to her grandson and nodded her approval to approach Hanbo.

"Hanbo?"

"Yeah, Hanbo."

Kureo unloaded her suitcase and sat on the threshold opposite her son. She sighed and dropped a blank gaze on the dirt foyer.

"The four-*tatami* room behind the kitchen is empty. An old bureau is there, so use it," Nao said.

Motionless, Uruo watched these two new family members remove their footwear and head for the smallest room inside.

"Cousin Hanbo," Uruo muttered to himself. It seemed to Uruo as if his older brother had returned from a long journey.

Uruo walked over to the flower bed in the center of the backyard and stood before the large brown faces of sunflowers encircled by petals like yellow flames. He touched a petal; it was warm, like his own fingers.

Uruo sprawled on the grass that surrounded the flower bed and looked up. The fathomless blue expanse enveloped him. He inhaled deeply until his chest swelled. The autumn air of the backyard, faintly tinted with the odor of chicken manure, tasted fresh. He held the air in as long as he could and then let it all out at once. He clasped his hands under the back of his head and let his vision melt into the enormous blue spread above.

Tiny specks of dust swirled in the space between Uruo's vision and the blue sky. They had no color, only countless shapes constantly shifting their positions. Some looked as if they were hopping around like crickets, others scurried evenly from left to right and back, and many busied themselves like tadpoles in the streams in the rice field near the Mitsukaidō pond where he went with Hanbo, now a high school sophomore waiting for the winter vacation. Uruo could not pinpoint what these little floaters were. He was unsure whether they were in his eyes or in the air.

A fluffy cloud floated into Uruo's view. *A dog's head!* he decided. The cloud did look like a side view of a dog with a bent ear, a thick nose line with a large marble-like muzzle, and with a short neck that faded into the blue air. The dog flew forward over the Mitsukaidō train station toward the sun that shone more gold now than it had in the morning.

Another cloud showed up, shapeless. He narrowed his eyes and focused on it. The cloud looked like a dandelion seed. But then it could be a hobgoblin with no face.

"Ah, a starfish!" Uruo could not hide the joy of pinpointing the shape of this cloud. His high-pitched voice echoed in the backyard. As if responding to Uruo, a crow croaked from the top of the persimmon tree that stood tall inside the brown wooden fence at the northeast corner of the backyard.

The starfish cloud, just like the dog cloud, passed by without changing its shape. Uruo was hoping it would turn like a pinwheel.

He blew hard at the starfish in the sky just like he, when he was a toddler, used to blow at the pinwheel that Nao had bought for him one summer night at the Bon festival of Zenchō-ji Temple where Uruo's school was located. But this starfish did not somersault. It followed the dog cloud, indifferent to Uruo.

The sky was blue and immense once again. Uruo rubbed his eyes. And, when he opened them, the tiny floaters returned to his vision. Uruo focused his sight on the largest floater of all. At that moment, the floater spurted a huge patch of ink like an octopus, taking away the blue expanse from him. He abruptly sat up, aware of his heart pounding inside his ears.

Then, there was no more ink, only the spotless sky. He breathed a sigh of relief that it was just a trick of his imagination again.

The voices of Mrs. Kon and the children wafted through his memory, inviting him to go to school with them.

Uruo had to figure out how to avoid them again the following morning.

March 1959

"HEY, YOU! Coal Boy!" Jōji yelled.

Uruo's knees jerked, destroying half of the little mountains and rice fields he had created in the sandbox for his wooden locomotive to pass by.

Standing on the top of the red-clay mound that was almost as high as the temple's roof, Jōji gave the illusion of a little giant. Uruo felt as if he were a midget.

"Come on, Coaly," Jōji yelled again, smirking while smacking down the other boys who had dashed up the mound to challenge him.

Some of the boys tumbled down the mound like crashing lumber. Others tottered, unable to keep balance. A group of boys congregated at the foot of the mound laughed at those who came rolling down the hill. They shoved one another to hurl defiance back at Jōji.

"Go for it, Coaly." A boy, who had his head shaven and had a face as round as a mooncake, pressed Uruo.

White heat ignited inside Uruo's stomach and it shot up into his brain. "Coaly" was a new insult.

Uruo did not know the name of this bald boy, but knew that he was Jōji's minion, endowed with a big mouth.

Many boys hid it, but they were afraid of Jōji Tange. Jōji was large for a seven-year-old, giving the false impression that he was confident and fearless. He had never lost a game of King of the Hill to the other boys, who felt honored when Jōji spoke to them in class and during breaks.

"Hey, what's the matter with you, Coaly?" Jōji said.

"Coaly is a girl," Jōji's bald lackey said.

The boys laughed.

Uruo destroyed the remaining mountains and valleys in the sandbox in one sweep of his right hand. He grabbed sand in both hands and glared at Jōji on the mound who was still thrusting away boys who challenged him. Uruo crouched and estimated the distance between the sandbox and the foot of the mound, and from there to the gentlest upward slope on the side of the mound facing the temple's main hall.

Sand stirred up behind Uruo. He darted the mound at full power, his eyes focused on Jōji's neck.

Jōji let go of the boy he was now grappling with. He lowered himself, opened his arms, and swiftly braced himself for Uruo's attack.

But Uruo did not attack Jōji: He dodged first to the right of Jōji and then to the left. Then Uruo threw the sand in his left fist at Jōji's eyes.

Jōji screamed and got a mouthful of sand from Uruo's right fist.

He choked as he tried to rub the sand out of his eyes. It stained his tongue and teeth as if sprinkled with brown sugar.

Jōji landed on his rear and rolled straight off the mound. For the first time. The boys heard Jōji cry.

Uruo wasted no time. He flew down the slope, grabbed Jōji, sat astride across his chest, and seized him by the neck. Uruo shook Jōji hard; Jōji's head hit the red-clay dirt. The boys around them, shocked and speechless, stepped back.

"Stop it, Uruo!" the temple gardener yelled, plowing his way through the boys. "Let him go."

Uruo strangled Jōji tighter, defying the gardener. The gardener jumped on Uruo from behind, grabbed him with his massive arms, and pulled him away from Jōji. Uruo elbowed at the gardener's abdomen ferociously. The gardener restrained his arms tighter, crouching down to steady himself as he held the struggling boy.

Jōji's scream had prompted Mrs. Kon to dash out of her classroom.

"What happened? You tell me what happened, Uruo." Mrs. Kon kneeled down before Uruo's shaking body.

Uruo wriggled himself out of the gardener's grip and spat on Mrs. Kon's face. With all his power, he thrust the gardener away from him and dashed to the temple's *torii* gate. The gardener staggered backward, nearly falling on the ground.

Jōji was still wailing and trying to get the remaining sand from his eyes. Realizing he was the only man who could carry a boy the size of Jōji, the gardener scooped him up to take him to the nurse's office located north of the five-story pagoda between the temple and the school of the temple grounds. Mrs. Kon trotted behind the gardener with Jōji in his arms.

"Jōji, tell me what happened," Mrs. Kon demanded.

"He's hurt, ma'am," the gardener said.

"I need to know what happened. Master Kangen is going to hear about this. And Jōji's mother—she is a board member."

When he arrived at the Mitsukaidō pond, Uruo was breathless and his mouth felt dry. Tears kept running down his cheeks. These extra salty tears were no help to his dry mouth. Uruo was still thinking about the temple's imposing, black-tiled roof that swept up toward the sky. He felt as though the roof was surging on to him from behind like a black tidal wave; no matter how fast he ran, the roof's sweep was behind him, threatening to swallow him up.

Uruo embraced the old cypress tree at the pond and pressed his left ear against its bark. He listened and thought he heard something moving, pulsating. He was not certain what he was hearing. Perhaps it was the water traveling up and down deep inside the tree. Perhaps it was some creatures gnawing the tree root underground. He noticed the tree's rugged roots spread out into the pond.

Uruo was still sobbing. A thread of pee leaked down his right leg and his wet front rubbed onto the bark. His whole body ached.

"Why am I not a tree?"

Uruo wanted someone to give him an answer—Nao, Cousin Hanbo … anyone, even Kureo who frightened him.

"Why can't I be a tree?" Uruo muttered again. "They just stand by the pond."

No voice answered him, just the deep mysterious sounds from the old cypress's trunk.

He let go of the tree. And, wiping the traces of pee off his leg with his hand, he stepped toward the water edge and sat cross-legged on the grass.

A green frog splashed into the pond. Ripples widened across the water toward the opposite bank. Uruo's eyes followed a ripple until it could no longer fan out.

The feverish energy that burned inside Uruo at the temple school had subsided. Despite the bright sun, goosebumps traveled from his wrists all the way up to his nape. Uruo folded his arms and stooped.

Casting a blank gaze at a water strider gliding on the pond's surface, Uruo wondered if he could even go home after what he did to Jōji. Mrs. Kon knew where he lived; she could have gone to his grandmother and reported the incident. Or worse, to Aunt Kureo. By now the whole town of Mitsukaidō might know that Uruo had blinded Jōji with sand and nearly choked him to death. Uruo had no idea how he had summoned such strength.

Nao had never witnessed Uruo turn violent. Neither had Hanbo. Nao always told Uruo that he was a decent boy, and that he had no reason to feel ashamed of his walnut-colored skin. But Uruo knew he was different from other children. The townspeople stared at him, cast sidelong glances, and whispered to one another.

His grandmother might refuse to let Uruo in the house. Hanbo might decide he no longer wanted to be Uruo's "big brother." If they were mad at him, he might have to stay at the pond overnight and decide what to do in the morning.

Uruo's sobbing went on as if it was shaking his chest on its own force. He let it go on. There was no reason to stop it. As he immersed himself in his own sadness, it occurred to him that he could sink all the way down to the bottom of the pond and stay there forever. It'd be better that way than having to live in the dark skin that seemed to grow darker by the day.

His right finger trembled as it traced his black left arm toward its wrist. He pinched his skin with two fingers, harder and harder. It hurt. But it was worth the pain if his fingers could peel the black skin off his arm. Then maybe white skin, like Hanbo's, might grow.

His left arm dropped like rubber. His right hand hung in the air. Beneath his right hand, half-buried in the ground near the water's edge, was a rainbow-colored stone, reflecting the evening glow. With his fingers, he dug up the stone. It was an abalone shell as big as his palm. He washed the shell in the pond. The rainbow-color brightened.

The left side of the shell was sharper than the right side. Uruo brought the sharp side of the shell down on his left arm and moved it back and forth between his elbow and wrist. He then gave more pressure to the abalone. The pain intensified as the shell scraped his skin.

"Show me my white skin." Fever ignited in his stomach, shot up into his throat, then into his eyes. Tears gushed out. A thin thread of red stained the sharp edge of the shell as Uruo stabbed it deeper into his skin.

"Ah!" Uruo's scream echoed through the wood around the pond. He drew backward, fell sideways, and threw the shell into the pond. He sat back on the grass cross-legged and glared at the blood seeping out of his arm. He then turned to the water. Lying on his stomach, he lowered his left arm into the water. The cold water took the fever out of his body. He gently covered the scraped wound with his undershirt.

Under the growing shadows of the trees on the east side, the pond was turning dark. His pants were damp, and the odor of piss was pricking his nose. Mosquitoes buzzed around him. Tiny black bugs landed on him and climbed up and down his arms. He brushed them off time and again; they kept coming back.

The bamboo grove behind the cypress tree rustled. The noise stopped.

Uruo pricked up his ears, looking around.

He heard the same noise again, though quieter than the previous one.

Crawling, and covering his left arm with his undershirt, Uruo moved closer to the thickest part of the cypress root that could fence in his small body. He held his breath.

There was a shadow squatting by the cypress trunk.

"I knew you were here," the shadow whispered.

"Hanbo … Cousin Hanbo." Uruo threw himself into Hanbo's arms.

March 1959

Wiping sweat off his forehead with his stained apron, Gen came out to the entrance of his bakery.

"Going to be a warm day."

"I don't know how you spend all day in that back room baking stuff." Nao, accompanied by Uruo, strode over the doorsill of the entrance and came into the store. "Do you have some bread crusts for us?"

"Of course."

"Thank you, Mr. Gen." She leaned over the counter.

"Don't mention it, Mrs. Yusa."

"I am thankful."

"Now." Gen addressed Uruo. "I have something for you. Why don't you sit there on the mushroom?" Gen watched as Uruo went to the corner at the end of the counter and sat on the mushroom-shaped stool placed in front of the window.

Uruo turned the stool left and right as he had done so every time he sat on it, turning it faster and faster.

Gen brought Uruo a wax paper bag.

"Here. Your favorite bread." Gen pinched Uruo's cheek. "Open it."

Uruo looked up at him, opened the bag and peeked inside. "*Anpan*! Oh, Uncle Gen, thank you." Uruo took out a round, shiny bread and took a big bite out of it. "So sweet."

"I baked it this morning just for you and stuffed it with a lot of red bean paste."

Gen returned to the other side of the counter where Nao was looking at a new list of sweets on sale that day.

"Anything you'd like to take home?"

"I wish I could, but I've lost two teeth this year. Can't afford to lose any more." Nao turned to Uruo and then back to Gen.

"By the way, have you heard the rumor?" Gen lowered his voice.

"What rumor?"

"The water goblin that showed up in the Mitsukaidō pond."

"No, I haven't heard anything of the sort. I've lived in this town most of my life, but never heard of any water goblin. They must be kidding."

"Some people saw the goblin."

"Who in the world would believe such nonsense, Mr. Gen?"

"The townspeople are talking about it."

The rumor made no sense to Nao. Why would the townsfolk talk about such an imaginary creature that only existed in old Japanese folklore? Nao was certain someone joked about a *kappa*, and the joke got spread. But then Gen seemed serious about the rumor; he insisted some people had seen the creature. She frowned at him and dropped her gaze on a crack of the concrete floor that resembled a bolt of lightning.

Gen disappeared into the back room and returned with a teapot and two small teacups. He put them on the table near the counter and offered her a wooden chair with hardly any varnish left on it. He seated himself across from her.

With reverence she bowed to the green tea Gen had served, drew in the leafy scent of the tea, and took a sip. She nodded to him her gratitude and approval.

"Jōji's nine-year-old sister, Tae, and three of her friends were passing through the woods surrounding the pond," Gen said. "There is a narrow path running through there, a shortcut to and from Mitsukaidō Elementary School. Kids sometimes play there, pretending that ghosts chase them around.

"That day, after school, the kids were on their way home through the woods. Suddenly, Tae stopped and pointed to the pond. She could not speak. The other girls froze up at the sight of what Tae's finger was pointing at.

"A *kappa,* Mrs. Yusa. That's what the girls said they saw. The *kappa* was dark-skinned, not green, Tae said. The girls were not sure if this *kappa* had a small saucer on top of his head, you know, to keep its water in. Water goblins gain terrific strength on land when their saucers are filled with water. But if the water evaporates or spills over, they are left debilitated."

Gen held the teacup with both hands and peeked into the tea as if looking for something lost. A tea stalk was floating erect. He smiled and lowered his voice further:

"This *kappa* had fluffy hair. I thought water goblins are supposed to have dirty spiky hair, like pine needles. It's so scanty you can see the saucer. Strange, isn't it? The *kappa* was rubbing his arms with a pumice stone while he chanted an incantation. Blood oozed out of his arms, and his chanting turned into sobbing. The girls got so frightened they ran away as fast as they could."

"Interesting, Mr. Gen. Kids are the greatest story tellers, in my opinion. They can see things we adults can't. They've got rich imaginations."

"But this one is bizarre enough to frighten the whole town."

"They are just playing along, I am sure. For a quiet town like ours, anything can become an event." Nao turned to Uruo who was watching Namiki Street through the window. Fluffy hair, dark skin. Uruo did sometimes wash himself hard with a dry loofah until she told him to stop it. Never with a pumice stone, though.

Nao wondered if it was Uruo that Tae saw. If so, why was he at the pond at that time of the day? These thoughts ran wild in Nao's head.

"More tea?"

Gen's gentle offer startled Nao, her back straightening itself. She bowed.

After their late morning tea at the bakery, Nao and Uruo left the shop. On the way home, Uruo munched on the second *anpan* that Gen had given him. Nao had a bagful of bread crusts in her hand basket. Her free hand kept ruffling Uruo's curly black hair as if to convince herself that her grandson had no saucer on top of his head.

"Are we going to eat the bread tonight for dinner, Grandma?"

"Too early to talk about dinner. Finish your *anpan*."

"This one is bigger than the first one."

"I don't know why Mr. Gen loves you so much. He used to hold you in his arms when you were a baby. Once you peed all over his chest. You don't remember it, do you?"

"I still wet my pants … sometimes."

A gentle tittering escaped from Nao's nose.

"Do you want me to carry your basket?"

"If you want to, son."

The handbasket seemed suddenly larger in Uruo's hand. It nearly touched the dirt road. Uruo ran his left palm along the bottom of the basket and tossed it on to his back, gripping the handles with his right hand. He smiled to himself for this clever idea of handling the basket.

A woman in a purple *kimono* with a pattern of plum blossoms, a pair of white *tabi*, and a pair of black lacquered wooden clogs, appeared from the west side of Meigetsu Street, about ten meters ahead of Nao and Uruo. She was coming toward them, heading for the train station. Uruo dropped his glance to the flapping of her *kimono* hem that showed a shiny cream lining. Her wide silver *obi*, covering her chest down to her waist, reflected the sun like a sheet of thin metal. She did not stop. She greeted Nao: "Good day, Mrs. Yusa," parting her bright red lips, showing her front teeth tinged with the color of her lips. Uruo tried to recall things he had eaten that might have stained his teeth red. He did remember wild strawberries, blueberries, raspberries, wild goumi he and Hanbo had picked and eaten in the wild grass near the rice paddy fields. But none of them dyed his teeth bright red.

"Likewise, Mrs. Tange." Nao bowed to her, not directly facing her.

Uruo shifted the basket from his right shoulder to his left shoulder and looked back to see the woman's silver drum knot of *obi* fastened on her back.

Uruo slowed down. The woman was in the middle of the road, half turned, staring at both Nao and Uruo.

"She is watching us, Grandma," Uruo whispered and pulled Nao's sleeve.

"I know," Nao said. "She has done it many times before. Don't pay attention to her."

"Is she mad at us?"

"No. She feels uncomfortable around us."

"Uncomfortable? Why?"

"She thinks we are different." Nao patted Uruo's left shoulder, urging him to turn around. "Come now. Let's go home."

Nao heard the water pump squeaking. Hanbo, dressed only in a loincloth after raking together the chicken manure in the hencoop, squatted inside the stone enclosure around the well. He was rinsing out the soap from a pair of black pants which he had worn while he cleaned up the hencoop that day. He had worn this same pair for the past two years to go to school.

"I will get you a clean pair of pants." Nao turned around and went back to the house through the kitchen entrance and came back out with a pair of thin short pants made of cotton in her hand.

Hanbo hooked the pants up on the pump handle and removed his loincloth with ease.

"My oldest grandson is becoming a man," Nao whispered to herself. She sighed and gazed at Hanbo's wide shoulder line that tapered down to small muscular buttocks from which extended a pair of short sturdy legs.

"When you are done changing, come over to the veranda," Nao said. "We will slice some pickled gherkin. I'll collect the eggs later."

Hanbo brought a small pail of water with a thin bamboo ladle to the veranda where Nao had already begun picking at the pickle slices with her chopsticks. He took one slice out of the saucer with his fingers and tossed it into his mouth. He then gave a grunt of approval to the pleasant taste of the sweet vinegar that soaked the gherkin slice.

"I want to ask you something." Nao threw a quick glance at Hanbo.

"It's about the *kappa* at the pond, isn't it?"

Nao nodded and said, "How do you know?"

"Everybody in town knows, Grandma."

"I suppose so." She picked up another slice of sour-sweet, pickled gherkin. "Who did you talk to?"

"Mr. Oppuri?"

"What were you doing there in his house?"

"Helping him fix his roof. He pays me good."

"That's good to know. But what did he say? A dark-skinned *kappa* rubbing his arm with a stone? Blood coming out of his arms?"

"All that."

"Did you say anything to him?"

"I told him the *kappa* was my cousin. These girls didn't see me from the path in the wood because I was behind the cedar tree."

"Wait. Were you with Uruo at the pond that day?"

"Uruo didn't come straight home that afternoon, you remember? I knew something had happened. I went to the pond because I know he loves it there. We've been there several times together before. Anyway, I found him sitting on the cedar root."

"And?"

"He told me what happened at the school. You know—the fight with Jōji?"

Nao nodded.

"Jōji is the instigator—he bullied Uruo. Uruo defended himself."

"I never knew he could defend himself alone," Nao said in a tone that sounded at once solemn and proud.

"He got mad as hell, Grandma."

"The school's kids have said nasty things to Uruo since he started going there."

"You let him stop going to school, didn't you?"

"I had no choice, Hanbo. You and I can't imagine the pain he's been going through—and he is only seven years old." Nao's chewing noise suddenly turned louder and faster. She scooped a ladleful of water from the pail, sipped it twice, and let out a sigh. "Jōji's father, Mr. Tange, is the head of the town assembly," Nao murmured.

Hanbo knew that a man of Tange's standing could quiet the rumor, or else he could fuel it with vengeance. Hanbo braced himself for whichever path Tange might choose but feared for the worst.

April 1959

NAO SMELLED like a mothball that morning. And the smell pervaded the whole house. It made Uruo anxious to see his grandmother in her formal clothes. Nothing good ever happened when she wore those.

Uruo's gaze followed Nao's gray formal *kimono.* His fingers kept tracing the hem of his new pair of black pants Nao had bought for him to wear that day. Uruo could not figure out what was happening in the house. His curiosity tinged with anxiety traveled back and forth between Nao's *kimono* and his new black pants.

Nao had not said much since she opened the sliding shutters of the veranda to let the morning sun into the house. Uruo was unhappy that she had ignored him all morning—even during breakfast. Hanbo carried the conversation. Kureo, as always, had her breakfast in her room, sitting at the knitting machine.

"Mr. Oppuri is going to pay me with rice when his roof is all fixed," Hanbo said.

"What do you mean 'pay me with rice'?" Uruo asked.

"I helped Mr. Oppuri so he is going to reward me by giving me some rice."

"Why rice?"

"Because that's what Mr. Oppuri can give."

"A good reward, indeed. It will help us a lot," Nao muttered, not looking at Hanbo or Uruo. "I'm grateful, Hanbo."

The pitch of Nao's voice signaled that she had been preoccupied with something. It did not take long for Hanbo to know what her preoccupation was. Hanbo decided not to ask her any questions that might agitate her. "Not a problem, Grandma."

"I want to fix our roof, Cousin Hanbo." Uruo was chewing hot rice mixed with shredded dry bonito. He scooped the rice into his mouth with chopsticks, wishing he were using a spoon instead.

"You can do that when you get to my age."

"That's too long."

"You can wait. Besides, you've got to know how to use tools and to measure things."

"I can bang with a hammer, right Grandma?"

She was sipping her miso soup, the soup bowl hiding most of her face.

"Good. I'll remember that. Next time I make something, like a shelf on the wall, I'll let you help me."

"Promise, Cousin Hanbo?"

"Promise."

The house fell silent.

Nao got up, gathered her bowls and chopsticks, and took them to the kitchen, ignoring both Uruo and Hanbo.

"Hurry up. Grandma is about to go out," Hanbo whispered to Uruo. "You have to go with her."

Her dishes made a dull noise against the wooden sink in the kitchen.

After he gulped down his miso soup, Uruo run into the vestibule and put on his canvas shoes.

Nao came around the house to the house gate from the kitchen back entrance and met Uruo. "We shouldn't be late, son?"

They went out to the street, Nao leading the way with quick steps. Uruo followed Nao stepping on stones that stuck out of the dirt road.

As they made a left on Namiki, Uruo stopped, throwing a resistant gaze at Nao's back. "No, I don't want to go there!" Uruo yelled at Nao. They were heading towards Zenchō-ji Temple's elementary school.

"You come with me, boy," Nao yelled back to him and gripped his arm tight. Uruo resisted. Nao pulled him along, almost dragging him.

He squatted on the dirt road. His sobbing swelled into an uncompromising shriek.

Nao abruptly forced him to stand up and shook him hard by the shoulder.

"All right. If you don't want to go to the school, go back to the pond. Hanbo won't be there for you this time. You hear me?"

Uruo's shriek reached its peak, and then quieted down. He looked at the direction of the pond, then looked into Nao's stern eyes.

She kneeled to him, pulled out a folded white handkerchief from underneath her light brown sash and unfolded it. She wiped his eyes with it. He frowned at the mothball smell.

"I am going to the school. If you want to stay here, you may." Nao walked away. Uruo wanted her to turn around and come and get him. She did not come back.

There was a large stone by the base of a telegraph pole at the southeast corner where Namiki and Meigetsu Streets intersected. The stone was trapezoidal and striped diagonally in white, cream, and black. Uruo walked over to the stone and bent over to touch the top of it. The surface was smooth. He felt it with two fingers, then with three, and finally with the palm of his hand. Uruo, fascinated by its shape and stripes, wanted to take this stone home, and put it by the flower bed or maybe in front of the persimmon tree in the backyard so that everybody could sit and look at the flowers, the bees, and the butterflies. But how could he carry it home?

Uruo pushed the stone, to see if it would move. The stone ignored him. Uruo stared at the stripes on the side of the stone. He kicked the stone with his heel. A pain ignited inside his heel, and it quickly spiraled up into his groin. He screamed and fell on the dirt road.

Uruo saw Nao's silhouette far ahead of the road, small and all gray. He thought he saw her stop for a moment, moved by his scream. But she didn't come back. He stood still and stared at her gray silhouette. Then, his hand in his pants pockets, he walked forward—reluctantly following Nao from far.

When Uruo removed his shoes at the base of the twelve-step stairway that led to the main hall of the Zenchō-ji Temple, the temple master Kangen was speaking to his grandmother. Uruo gripped the left railing with his hand, and he slowly ascended to the hall.

At the threshold into the hall, Uruo sat on his heels in formal manner. Placing both of his palms on the *tatami* mat, he gave a deep bow to show his respect, although he did not know for whom he deep-bowed.

"I am glad you are here, Uruo." Master Kangen's serene voice resonated.

Uruo took Master Kangen's words as permission to raise his head and return to his straight posture.

The faces of Master Kangen, Mrs. Kon, Jōji, his mother, and the temple gardener surged into Uruo's vision all at once, like spears flying at him from all directions.

"Come sit here by me." Nao pushed the cushion forward between herself and the gardener.

Tracing the deep green cloth hemming that defined each of the *tatami* mats, Uruo arrived at where the cushion was placed, and sat by Nao. The floor cushion was twice as thick and comfortable as the ones at home.

Uruo's gaze clashed with Jōji's.

Jōji averted his eyes from Uruo.

Uruo kept his stare fixed on Jōji, while at the same time overwhelmed by lavender perfume drifting from Jōji's mother.

"Mrs. Tange, please continue," Kangen said.

"As I was saying," Mrs. Tange said, shaking her head priggishly. "My husband and I have never taught Jōji to bully his classmates. He is obedient and quiet at home. He is a model child. It is unthinkable that my son would bully your grandson, Mrs. Yusa."

"Uruo simply retaliated, so I understand."

"Retaliated for what?" Mrs. Tange raised her voice, her nose pointing upward.

"Jōji's remarks against Uruo," the gardener said. He kept his head low, but his voice reverberated in the hall. "He called Uruo 'Coal Boy' in front of all other children."

"Why, Mr.—whoever you are. How dare could you say such nonsense in public!"

"Could you offer any proof, Mr. Endō?"

"I was there when it all happened, Master Kangen. I was the one who took Jōji to the nurse's office, to have his eyes washed out. Mrs. Kon was with me."

Mrs. Kon looked at Master Kangen and, closing her eyes, nodded her agreement with the gardener Endō.

Mrs. Tange looked at her son, "Well?"

"I didn't say anything to him, Mama. He threw sand at me."

Uruo saw that Jōji was close to tears. "Jōji called me 'Coaly'. He called me 'Coal Boy' many times before, too. Because I am dark."

Uruo's unusually aggressive tone startled Nao. She now believed how violently Uruo had retaliated against Jōji.

"Mrs. Tange, do you believe the kind of boy who plays alone in a sandbox would have attacked your son for no reason at all?" Kangen asked.

"Well, anything could happen—as my husband always says."

"Facts differ from rhetoric, Mrs. Tange," Kangen said.

"What are you saying, Master Kangen?"

"This school prohibits bullying. The facts indicate that your son instigated an act of bullying which caused the incident."

"I am aware of the school's rules and regulations."

"You must be. You are our board member."

Mrs. Tange gasped, her right hand across her chest.

Nao did not hide her faint sarcastic smile when Uruo turned to her with a blank face.

Mrs. Kon and the gardener Endō looked at each other and turned to Master Kangen at the same time.

"I must be going. My time is precious, as my husband would say." Mrs. Tange picked up her light purple purse that matched her *kimono* with its patterns of plum blossoms. She bowed to Master Kangen. She then stood up and marched toward the threshold of the hall, her *tabi* brushing against the *tatami* floor. "You will hear from my husband's office."

Jōji followed.

The calls of the bush warblers in the wood crescendoed, then subsided.

"Mrs. Kon, Mr. Endō, you may return to your duties."

Mrs. Kon came over to Uruo with a small box in her hand, knelt down by him, and opened the box. "Your locomotive, Uruo."

He took the toy and bowed to Mrs. Kon who, in turn, touched his cheek and nodded a few times.

Mrs. Kon followed Mr. Endō out onto the stairway down.

"Mrs. Yusa, in a few days, Mr. Endō will deliver to you in person some documents." The Master paused. He looked into Nao's eyes. "The package will include a picture clipped from the *Asahi News* that may be of great interest to you. Let me help, if you will, Mrs. Yusa."

Nao's unyielding gaze collided with Master Kangen's. Since the day Uruo assaulted Jōji—the son of an assemblyman—he had sensed someone would attempt to intervene about Uruo. How they would do so remained unknown.

Two days after the meeting with Master Kangen, the gardener Mr. Endō delivered to Nao a package bearing Zenchō-ji Temple's seal. Nao invited Endō in for a cup of coarse tea. But he declined her offer as he was on duty and had to return to the temple. Endō bowed with reverence and left the house.

Nao sat at the dinner table and stared at the unopened envelope. The commanding presence of the Zenchō-ji seal on the envelope gave her shivers. It sucked moisture out of her throat at the same time. She swallowed over and over. She got up, went to the kitchen, and ladled some cold water out of the clay pot under the sink. Returning to the dinner table in the eight-*tatami* room, she felt her heartbeat accelerate. From a box of sewing tools that she kept by the bureau with the house altar on top of it, she picked up a pair of small scissors. She gazed at the envelope and the scissors in turn and then cut the top of the envelope, slowly and ceremoniously.

The envelope contained a small picture and a two-page letter in calligraphic cursive style with Master Kangen's signature and his red seal. In the center of the picture stood a tall woman with a short black hair, with a learned smile on her large octagonal face. Surrounding this woman were a dozen children about five or six years old—some were dark-skinned like Uruo, and others were lighter. The children had one thing in common: They all looked foreign.

The letter from Master Kangen detailed that the picture represented the children of St. Veronica's Home and its founder. This institution for displaced biracial children received financial support both from the American Episcopalian Association and from the Anglican Humanitarian Society in Great Britain. The institution provided the children with food, room, and medical care while they received nine years of basic education. The letter concluded that, considering Uruo's racial background and the townspeople's reaction to it, as well as the Yusa family's hardships, sending Uruo to this Christian institution with international connections would seem the best solution for him and for his future.

Nao let out a deep sigh and rested her chin in her hand. Nine years of education—this issue captivated Nao's attention. But she resented Master Kangen advising her what could be the best for her. He had no authority to do that to her. It then occurred to her that sending Uruo to the institution sounded too benevolent, too good to be true. It could be a scheme—Nao suspected. It could be the Tange family's tactic to expel her grandson—the black-skinned troublesome seed—from Mitsukaidō. This way Mitsukaidō could return to a peaceful rural town it once was. But then what would this scheme make Master Kangen? Certainly not a revered Buddhist priest. Ambivalence clouded Nao's thoughts. Betrayal eradicated her trust in this town she had spent most of her life. And a sense of defeat violated her pride. She placed the picture and the letter back in the envelope and laid it in front of the house altar on the bureau. She joined her hands and bowed to the altar, but she did not pray to her ancestors for help.

"No! They haven't crushed me yet," Nao spat out a whisper. If Uruo would enter the Christian institution, he would have good food, good place to live, friends of his own kind, and above all decent education until he would turn fifteen years old. "The victory is in my hand, Mr. Tange, and Master Kangen!" Nao's ashen face suddenly flashed.

June 1960

WAITING IRRITATED Uruo. But that afternoon, leaning against the bamboo fence outside the Mitsukaidō train station, Uruo was eager to wait for the arrival of a train.

He had no idea if the train was coming from the south or from the north. But he did know one of the two pairs of railroad tracks would take him to a place called Tokyo, located far away from Mitsukaidō. Cousin Hanbo had spoken of his dream of going to Tokyo to work for a corporation after graduating from high school in two years. When he shared his dream with Uruo, Hanbo's face lit up with hope and anticipation, which, in turn, brought on the possibility Uruo might lose his big brother. On the other hand, two years seemed to Uruo long ahead. He hardly grasped how long two years might be. Hanbo's departure to Tokyo remained only a hazy image for him. Hanbo was his brother for now.

Uruo folded his arms over the bamboo fence and rested his head on them. He narrowed his eyes, facing the east and focusing on the farthest distance where two mountain ridges overlapped to hide a valley between them. The two tracks gradually bent rightward and disappeared into the valley. When Hanbo would one day go to Tokyo, his train would follow this long curvature of the tracks. The steam engine would make rough noise in perfect unison with the back-and-forth motion of the piston, belching out massive amounts of soot from its funnel.

A thin whistle cut through the cicadas' chorus reverberating in the summer air.

Uruo craned.

A second whistle blew thicker and louder than the first. A pillar of soot arose from the valley, splitting the cloudless sky in two, and then gradually melted into haze. In a short while Uruo could see the front face of the steam engine with the soot gushing out of the funnel as it chugged wildly. A long line of passenger cars appeared from the valley, defining the leisurely curve of the rail toward the Mitsukaidō train station. When the steam engine shifted westward onto the straight tracks, Uruo marveled at its huge face, its enormous energy. The mechanical smell of the soot captivated him and elicited a sense of anticipation toward the future.

The crossing bell rang above Uruo's head, and the pole came down to close the crossing. Gradually slowing down, the steam engine made its majestic entry into the station.

He waved at the passengers in the cars that had slid into the platform. No passengers returned Uruo's welcome.

Just then, a sandpaper-like sensation scraped Uruo's ankles. He turned and froze for a second at the size of the dog that was now looking at him, wagging its curled-up tail. Uruo at once saw that the dog was smiling at him. He let the dog smell his fingers. The dog licked them, then stood up on his hind legs, and licked his chin. The dog's sandpaper tongue tickled Uruo's walnut skin. He hugged the dog as if by instinct. Excited, the dog wagged its tail harder than before and kept licking Uruo's small face.

"Gosh, aren't you afraid of him?"

The voice startled Uruo. When he looked around, he found a girl standing behind him. "Is he yours?" Uruo asked.

The girl wore a pastel blue short-sleeved blouse and a pair of baggy navy-blue pants. "Yeah. His name is Jun-wan. Four years old. My dad got him from somebody at work. A shepherd."

"Stop licking," Uruo said to the dog.

Knowing he was spoken to, Jun-wan emitted a series of tender howls, with his muzzle pointing to the sky and his ears flat against his skull.

"Jun-wan likes you, um—"

"Uruo. Uruo Yusa."

"I'm Chisa Suda." She patted her left thigh a few times. Jun-wan first sniffed at Chisa's fingertips, exhaled on them as if to dismiss them, then sat by her, and let her put the leash around his neck. "I've seen you before, Uruo. You were here with a stocky guy."

"That's Hanbo, my cousin. His mom and my Grandma—we all live together. Hanbo goes to high school. We come here a lot to watch the train."

"Let's watch the train together—maybe tomorrow?" Chisa said. "Come to my house first. Then we'll come here with Jun-wan."

"Okay." Uruo felt uneasy accepting Chisa's suggestion. He had never been invited to anything. Uruo instantly regretted saying yes to her.

But his suspicion did not last long as Chisa's vivacious voice carried on. "My house is at the corner of Namiki and Meigetsu streets. It's easy to find. Bamboo brooms always stand outside. Lots of them. And across from our shop is a funny looking stone right by the telephone pole."

"I know where it is. I'll be sitting on the stone if it's all right with you."

"Sure. I can see you from the shop."

Now leashed, Jun-wan came over to Uruo and sniffed his legs. Uruo crouched and scratched Jun-wan's ears while the dog licked Uruo's nose.

Chisa pulled the leash.

"Bye Jun-wan." Uruo leaned on the bamboo fence again.

Jun-wan barked once and seemed to smile at Uruo.

The next day, after breakfast, Uruo swept the row of stepping-stones that connected the bath-hut and the well to the kitchen entrance. It was his chore to perform. Afterwards, he switched from the soft broom to a hard bamboo one and ran to the vestibule of the house. The broom dug into the dirt floor of the vestibule like a steel brush. Nao always told him that the cleanliness of the floor welcomed whoever would visit the house that day: it showed the family's respect for the guests. Uruo made sure the horizontal trace of the broom's bristles were left across the dirt floor.

All this time Uruo kept hearing the mechanical noise coming from the four-*tatami* room. As always, the noise had precise intervals, punctuated by low twitters of chickens in the coop outside the room. With her forehead furrowed, her eyes triangular and her shoulders stooped, Aunt Kureo always wore the same *kimono* patterned with red, yellow, brown autumn leaves that had long faded into pale brown. Uruo suspected Aunt Kureo had no other clothes.

When she had arrived at the house, she only had a wicker suitcase and two wrapping-clothfuls of things. Uruo had not stepped into her room since then, but he wanted to. He wanted to see her smile at him, invite him in to sit on her lap, and tell him funny stories just as Nao had done since he was a toddler. But Uruo was not allowed in her room.

Leaning on the steps leading into the eight-*tatami* room, Uruo peeked at Aunt Kureo's room. The sliding door was half open. The sun light filled the room. The knitting machine kept on making its grating noise.

He gave a gentle sweep over the dirt floor one last time, following his grandmother's instruction.

When Uruo arrived at the trapezoidal stone, Chisa and Jun-wan were at Meigetsu Street. From his vantage point, Uruo could see two elderly women inside the store speaking to each other while looking at china bowls. The one in a navy-blue suit, holding a matching purse, pointed her finger at a large bowl, its edge a wavy shape.

Jun-wan pushed his massive head into Uruo's stomach, then stood up on his hind legs and licked Uruo's face.

Uruo hugged Jun-wan's thick neck, rubbing his face against the dog's short soft fur.

"I hope you didn't wait long, did you?" Chisa sounded apologetic.

"Just got here."

"Ready to go now?"

"To the train station?" Uruo stood up. "Or, maybe, the rice fields on the hill?"

"Oh, yeah, let's go to the hill."

At the top of the hill, Chisa unleashed Jun-wan and sat cross-legged on the grass. Uruo stretched his legs and watched Jun-wan zigzagging down the foot paths between paddies.

"Those are huge." Chisa's eyes widened at Uruo's bare feet. "How big are they?"

"I don't know. Grandma buys my stuff." Uruo removed his sandals. "Yours aren't that small, either."

Chisa removed her sandals and placed her feet next to Uruo's. "Now they match mine. I'm big for a girl."

"I'm still big for my age, I guess."

"You go to the school? I mean, the temple elementary?"

"I used to, but I don't anymore." Uruo's throat tightened. "How about you?"

"Mitsukaidō Elementary. I'm in eighth grade." Chisa's questioning gaze stayed on Uruo. "Why did you quit?"

Uruo wanted to run home and hide in the *futon* closet. "Because I'm different, you know?"

"No, you are not."

"Yes, I am. Look." Uruo placed his left arm by Chisa's right arm, and whispered: "See?"

He looked at their arms together closely. Uruo's was indeed darker, but not as dark as he thought. Chisa's skin was a dark tan, much darker than the other children in town. He blinked hard to make sure he wasn't imagining it, but it was real.

Both Uruo and Chisa turned to the slope of the terraced paddies at the same time. The terrace widened gradually as it spread downward toward the railroad tracks that ran cutting through the valley. The tracks reflected the sun like silver.

They said nothing.

Chisa held her crossed ankles with her hands, her eyes following each terraced paddy before her. "You come here often?" Chisa turned to Uruo.

"Yeah. Me and Hanbo like to watch the train from here. Sometimes we catch crayfish over there at the small field." Uruo pointed to east of the hill.

"Crayfish?"

"Yeah, crayfish."

"What do you do with them?"

"Eat."

"You can eat them things?"

"Sure. Grandma cooks them good. Cousin Hanbo can pick their meat real fast."

"Can you do that, too?"

"Not as fast as him."

Jun-wan returned and plunked down between Chisa and Uruo, fawning on them with his smiley face. His tail kept slapping the grass.

Uruo patted Jun-wan's wide forehead. "You never ate crayfish?"

"No. I didn't even know you could catch them in rice fields."

"Next time why don't you come with us?"

"Your cousin won't mind?"

"Oh, no."

Chisa fell silent. "Can I ask something?"

Uruo nodded at her, though he hoped it would not be about his skin color.

"Is your cousin good to you?"

"Why?"

"No reason. Just wondered."

"I love Hanbo. He's my big brother."

Chisa's gaze was gliding aimlessly across the mountain ridges. "I kinda thought so when I saw you two at the train station a while ago."

"You'll like him."

Jun-wan abruptly got up and sat at attention, his ears erect, and his eyes focused on the north end of the valley.

"What's the matter?" Chisa scratched Jun-wan's head, but Jun-wan shook her hand off at once and gave a low bark.

An aggressive rhythmic noise trembled the air across the mountain ridges, spoiling the stillness of the valley. With a hollowed whistle and the subsequent echo, the face of the steam engine popped into view.

"Look, Chisa." Uruo sprang up and pointed down the valley.

"I smell the smoke." Chisa stood up, awed at the gigantic black machine charging forward, pulling along a line of passenger cars.

The steam engine whistled again, louder and shriller than before.

"I bet this train came from Tokyo," Uruo said.

"This is great, Uruo—I mean, it's like looking at the train from the sky." Chisa's gaze penetrated the steam engine charging through the valley.

"Cousin Hanbo wants to go to Tokyo when he graduates from high school." His eyes traced the soot floating in the air. "I'm going with him."

Chisa was silent.

With the last passenger car disappearing south beyond the forest, serenity returned to the valley.

July 1960

IT CAME from the smallest of the three *tatami* rooms in the house again—a creaking heard at exact intervals. Some days the noise continued late into the night. The sliding-screen of this room had been kept shut while the creaking went on. This monotone noise irritated Uruo.

On one mid-summer day, in the late morning, Uruo saw the door of the small room cracked open and the sun casting its beam on the faded corridor and into the eight-*tatami* room. There Hanbo sat at a low dining table, with his legs stretched underneath it, working on his summer homework due in September when the second semester would commence at high school.

Lying on his stomach behind Hanbo, with a worn-out floor cushion folded under his chest, Uruo was glancing through a picture book his mother had brought home from Tokyo long time ago. His reading was not fluent. But he found it interesting that the letters in this book read sideways from left to right while the things Hanbo and Nao read had their letters set in an up-down and right-to-left fashion. Uruo preferred to ignore the words and focus on the images. Every time he opened this book, those colorful pictures charmed him into creating his own story.

But that morning Uruo's imagination did not last long enough to finish his new story. He was distracted by the open sliding-screen of the small room. It stirred up his curiosity. He closed the book and gazed at its cover picture: a blond girl in a blue one-piece and a white apron who was surrounded by lots of flowers in the woods, and a rabbit in a pair of dark green pants and a cream yellow coat with a bowtie looking askew at the girl. Uruo wondered where a girl or a boy with yellow hair like the one on the cover might live.

Kureo's machine kept creaking, and it distracted him from his thoughts. Uruo got up and tip-toed across the corridor and peeked into the small room.

His heart pounded twice. He quickly crouched outside the sliding-screen and peeked in the room once more. Aunt Kureo hunched over a long black shiny thing and was poking at a cloth-like square hanging from it; then she held a round knob attached to the top of the shiny thing and pushed it first to its left end and then back to where it was on the right side. She repeated this motion several times. She then poked at the hanging square again. Uruo stretched his neck to see what she was poking at. It was the same material as the sweaters stacked up by the bureau. Kureo was making a sweater like the one Nao gave him when the snow season arrived last year.

Uruo recognized that the noise came from this object in Kureo's room. He wanted to find out for himself what it looked like up close and why it creaked.

"Auntie, may I come in?"

Kureo jerked: Uruo's soft voice frightened her. She turned to Uruo, her floor-cushion turning with her. "What do you want?" Kureo spat out in a quick shush.

Uruo froze.

"You are not welcome in this room. You are not my child."

"I wanted to see—"

"You have nothing to see here."

Uruo stood there, transfixed by her fierce stare. It reminded him of when she had first arrived in the house from Kagoshima—her terror-stricken distant eyes that disapproved of Uruo, the son of her younger sister Aoi.

Uruo anticipated her next icy remark. A moldy odor mixed with sour taste suspended in the air and teased his nose. He rubbed his nose with the back of his hand.

"Get out," Kureo said. "You are not allowed in here. Hear me?"

"I am sorry, Auntie."

"Shut the screen."

Uruo closed the sliding screen, slowly, not to make any noise. He dashed away from the corridor into the kitchen and out into the backyard.

"Hanbo, what kind of machine is Auntie using?"

Hanbo confirmed that it was a knitting machine to make sweaters, and that the sweaters Aunt Kureo had made would be exchanged for half a straw bagful of rice at the Mitsukaidō market. The rice might last a month or so for the whole family, Hanbo estimated.

"Want to go to the paddy fields?" Hanbo asked.

"Oh yes!" Uruo's voice was so jovial that Kureo might have heard it in her room. "For crayfish?"

"Yeah."

"Piggyback, Hanbo." Uruo stood on tiptoe and stretched his arms as high as he could, his hazel eyes bright, showing his uneven teeth.

"You're getting a little too big for this, but okay." Hanbo laughed. He turned Uruo around, held the boy's waist with his hands, and tossed him up over his shoulders.

Uruo let out a shrill laugh and covered Hanbo's eyes.

"Don't do that, I can't see." Hanbo grabbed Uruo's hands and repositioned them across his forehead. Holding Uruo's leg in his left hand, Hanbo picked up a bucket with the other hand. He chose a shortcut to the paddy fields. No one passed by them.

At the paddy field, the sun was right above Uruo's head. Hanbo brought Uruo down and let him carry the empty bucket. Hanbo smiled and ruffled Uruo's curly hair.

"I want to go to the paddy by the hill. Because I can see the trains from there," Uruo said.

"All right." Hanbo did not mind walking a little further to the farthest paddy field because that was where large colonies of crayfish lived. He also knew that this paddy had the cleanest water. The stream rang like a wind chime, which seemed to soften the intensity of the sun.

At the narrow ridge of the paddy, Hanbo removed his shoes and rolled his pant legs up to his knees. Uruo did not have to because he had a pair of short pants on—which he had worn all through the year, except when Nao washed them.

"Grab that bucket."

Uruo took his shoes off, held the bucket handle, dragged it into the stream, and filled it halfway with water. He stood in the stream, looking down at the way the water forked around his ankles and then came together again. The dark brown sand felt rough under the soles of his feet. Uruo liked the coarseness of the sand. Moving his feet like a chicken scratching a hole in the dirt, Uruo buried his feet in the sand. A glacial sensation hit his spine—the sand was colder than the stream.

Something jumped into the bucket. Uruo turned to it.

"That's a big one there," Hanbo pointed to the bucket.

Forgetting the cold sand, Uruo stepped over to the bucket and poked at the tail of a crayfish, making it jerk in the water. Then he grabbed its middle body and lifted it into the air. The crayfish curled its tail inward and opened its claws apart. Uruo quickly ran his left index finger along one side of the open claw. The crayfish almost clipped Uruo's finger. He tried it again, quicker this time. The reflex of the crayfish to nip at anything that came near the claws fascinated Uruo. But he disliked its fishy smell. He wrinkled his nose as he dropped the crayfish back in the bucket.

Hanbo threw two more crayfish in the bucket. They were smaller than the first catch. Uruo watched them creep about in the bucket water. Then he caught up with Hanbo who was bending down to the bottom of the ridge that the water had hollowed out, stirring crayfish caves with a piece of dead wood.

Uruo walked forward in the stream along the ridge opposite where Hanbo was. He knew that, in their caves, some crayfish aligned themselves parallel to the flow of the water; and that others buried their heads in the caves, only their tail fins floating outside the caves.

Uruo stopped. He could not believe what he was looking at: a crayfish larger than Hanbo's first catch. This crayfish was so transparent that its entrails could be seen. Curious, he squatted low, his butt nearly touching the stream. The stream rang louder.

The see-through crayfish, its tail swinging carefree, did not seem to sense Uruo's feet in the water. Uruo was not certain if he could catch this crayfish in one grab. He looked at his right palm, then at the crayfish's tail joint whose circumference seemed a bit rounder than the whole area of his palm. He tilted his right wrist outward and stretched the thumb and the index finger as wide as he possibly could. As he lowered his right hand close to the stream, the flow of the water kept changing the shape of the crayfish.

This disturbance reminded Uruo of the flame in the old stone burner in the kitchen which Nao used every day for cooking rice in her sooty cauldron. The round opening on the stone burner, where twigs and firewood were thrown in to keep the fire going, was large enough that Uruo could see the fire raging as if it were about to burst the stone burner. Listening to the ominous howling of the fire, he would sit flat on the dirt floor. Although he kept a distance away from the burner, he felt the hot blast. The fire was alive. It behaved violently, it danced evilly, it remained in flux. The harder Uruo focused on its wild movement, the deeper he felt drawn to this unfathomable beast.

To him this stream was like the fire in the burner—it had no real face. He brought his face near the surface of the water. At that moment he saw that his face blocked the silver reflection of the sun in the stream. The shape of the see-through crayfish stood out, except its head that was still hidden in the cave.

Uruo dipped his right hand in the water. Spreading his fingers, he remained still. Then, slowly, he positioned his hand directly above the tail joint of the crayfish.

His hand snatched at the prey, at once ramming it into the sand, nearly burying it.

"Hanbo, look!" Uruo waved the crayfish in the air.

"Good job."

"For Grandma."

"Too big for her, don't you think?" Hanbo chuckled.

"You can help her eat it. You're a stocky guy."

"Stocky!" Hanbo said, laughing. "Where did you get that word from."

"Oh, nowhere I guess. Chisa said that."

Uruo's high-pitched voice reverberated in the bright stillness of the paddy field.

~

Uruo had just brought out the four floor cushions from the closet and placed them around the dinner table when Nao, holding a large trayful of boiled crayfish piled up high, entered the main room in the house. The aroma of the bright red crayfish overpowered the scent of incense from the double-doored house altar holding four mortuary tablets.

"Bring the rice tub, will you?" Nao said.

With his eyes fixed on the red crayfish pile on the table, Uruo started to make his way to the kitchen.

"They look a lot different from earlier," he said.

"When they are cooked, they turn red, son." Nao kept filling bowls with miso soup. "Is that what you are wondering about?"

"They smell different."

"Salt, onion, and garlic—all mixed."

Uruo went in the kitchen and came back holding the round rice tub in his arms.

"Put it down here, son." Nao showed him a spot on the *tatami* right by her.

Uruo sat upright at the table to the right of Nao, folding his legs properly as he had always done when he had food at the table. He watched the crayfish pile while Nao filled four small rice bowls.

Hanbo came in through the main vestibule, kicking off his wooden clogs, and sat cross-legged across from Nao. He flattened out the crayfish pile with his chopsticks.

"Here it is," Hanbo said, digging out the largest one Uruo had caught.

"That's for you, Grandma," Uruo said.

Nao smiled and patted Uruo on the cheek. "You caught it. It's yours."

"He won't give up," Hanbo said.

"All right, then." Nao pointed her index finger at the thick tail stretching out of the collapsed pile. "You break it, give me half, and you take the other half. Now, go get your mother."

"She won't come out. Why don't I just make a plate and take it to her, like I always do?"

Nao said nothing. She filled another rice bowl and gave it to Hanbo, who put it on a tray with a small dish with six small tails that he had twisted off. She then held her rice bowl and picked up her chopsticks. Her eyes followed Hanbo crossing the corridor to his mother's room where the creaking of her knitting machine was coming from.

Uruo twisted his first crayfish to remove the tail, pulled its white meat out on the plate with the tip of tapered bamboo chopsticks. He then broke the claws and took out the meat. Uruo picked a small amount of the meat with his chopsticks, put it on rice, and crammed it into his mouth.

Nao added a few more pieces of meat to Uruo's plate. "Good?"

Uruo gave Nao a big nod.

Hanbo returned to the table and chopped up the large hunk of tail meat he had shared with Nao.

The creaking from the small room stopped. The sudden stillness amplified the cracking of crayfish shells around the table.

"Why doesn't Auntie ever eat with us?"

"She is too busy making sweaters, son."

"She doesn't want to be a freeloader," Hambo chimed in.

"She has no business thinking that way," Nao said. "She was born and grew up in this house before she got married and went to Kagoshima. Her maiden name is Yusa like mine, Aoi's and her son's, you know?"

"Pride, Grandma, pride. My father was a career military officer."

"You talk about pride? Uruo's mother was so proud a woman she hardly talked about her life in Tokyo. And, and …" Nao covered her moth quickly as her chest heaved for a second.

Uruo cast a worried glance at Hanbo.

"It's the crayfish. It got stuck in my chest. You gave me a big piece of the tail, Hanbo. Take this end piece."

"Grandma." Hanbo's voice turned pensive. "You started saying something … about Uruo's mom?"

"Did I do anything bad to Auntie?" Uruo asked.

Nao put her chopsticks down on the plate. And, turning to Uruo, she said, "Come here, son."

She held him.

Hanbo watched as tears welled up in Nao's eyes.

Kureo's knitting machine creaked and then intensified, ignoring all that was happening in the house.

September 1960

HANBO HAD told Oppuri the truth that day: What the townsfolk called "*kappa*" was his cousin Uruo. Never did Hanbo think Oppuri would be the one to fuel the *kappa* rumor in town. Hanbo had expected Assemblyman Tange to do the broadcasting if anybody were to assume this task. Hanbo made a quick decision to stay away from Oppuri. But then Oppuri was, along with his daily newspaper delivery, a major source of Hanbo's income, even if Oppuri paid him in rice. Hanbo had no choice but to continue helping Oppuri with his carpentry. His inner turmoil on whether survival or integrity mattered more plagued him for days following the incident. The moment to make his decision once and for all arrived on a bright September day.

Hanbo and Uruo headed north on Namiki Street to get to Mitsukaidō Station. They were going to get an eastbound train to go to the adjacent station and take the next westbound train back to Mitsukaidō—a roundtrip about forty minutes. Uruo enjoyed sticking his neck out of the train's open window and feeling the strong wind against his face created by the steam engine that pulled twelve passenger cars. When the train followed the track that formed a sweeping curve and displayed a long leisurely half-circle, the fast-moving steel piston in coordination with a thick wad of soot fascinated Uruo. He studied the semi-circular motion of the piston and how this motion could push the gigantic black machine forward so fast. He wanted to sit in the driver's seat inside the locomotive and see how fast trees, houses, and rice fields would split apart at the face of the locomotive as it ran forward. This was Uruo's favorite pastime. He even dreamed of becoming a train conductor when he grew up.

Hanbo and Uruo were passing by the trapezoidal stone across from Chisa's general store when a hoarse voice caught their attention. "A brown *kappa*, Mitsukaidō's local attraction that no one wants to see. Go back to the pond where you belong."

Uruo swiftly turned around and then stepped back at the sight of a man behind them. The man had a diamond-shaped face and gray eyebrows. His left eye was white with no pupil—it looked as if a cloth ball had been pushed into his eye socket. The stained khaki military cap he wore had a visible tear above his right ear. Uruo saw a cruelty on the man's face that reminded him of Jōji. It ignited the unforgotten rage in Uruo, and he braced himself, looking for sand to throw in this man's good eye. But there was no sand to grab on the hardened dirt road of Namiki Street which he had walked countless times.

"C'mon little *kappa.* You can't even talk, can you?"

Hanbo towered in front of the man, getting between him and Uruo. "Why do you have to say that to a seven-year-old boy?" Hanbo paused. "Why?" He asked again. "Look at your dirty yellow skin. You haven't washed yourself for months. Don't you ever touch this boy. He is my cousin."

"That makes you a member of the Mitsukaidō *kappa* family, doesn't it?"

Hanbo thrust the man's chest with both hands.

The man fell on the pavement and writhed, his puttees-covered left leg as if numb. He raised his upper body and leaned forward and crawled toward the fire hydrant about six feet away.

The man clambered onto the fire hydrant to stand up. He looked back, throwing a glacial stare at Uruo. Spit shot out of his mouth. He limped along, his left leg rubbery, only its toes touching the ground.

Uruo studied the diagonal view of the lame man.

"My father used to dress like that," Hanbo said. "He was a soldier. He used to carry a sword, though."

"Did he kill anyone with it?"

"I don't know."

"Why does he dress like that?" Uruo's finger pointed at the man limping toward Meigetsu Street.

"I've seen him at the train station a few times. Every time I see him, he is standing on the east side of the station, by the public toilet. People give him money."

"He's a beggar?"

"Yeah, a beggar in a soldier's uniform."

"He was a soldier?"

"Maybe. Until the war ended. Then he couldn't get a job."

"His eye didn't move. It was scary." By now Uruo felt his rage subside into pity. "He looked sad though. Don't you think, Hanbo?"

"No, Uruo. Show him no mercy. He called you brown *kappa*."

"He was brown himself, wasn't he?"

"That was layers of dirt on his skin. He smelled awful, like piss."

The limping man disappeared.

"Uruo, you are not the only one with dark skin. You know that girl who lives at the corner of Meigetsu and Namiki Streets. She's dark, too. Her dad is even darker."

Uruo's almond shaped hazel eyes sparked. "Her name is Chisa, Hanbo. And she's thirteen now. An eighth grader at Mitsukaidō Elementary." He paused. "They don't call her Coal Girl, do they?"

"No. But some boys call her *Shiitake*, I hear."

"Why?"

"*Shiitake* mushrooms are brown."

"Is she okay with that?"

"She doesn't care. She runs after the boys, chases them away." Hanbo laughed. "She is a tough girl."

Uruo had a thought. "Why don't we bring her with us to the train station next time? She'll be happy to, Hanbo."

~

When Uruo opened a sliding glass door of Chisa's family's store, four bamboo brooms fell on Uruo and bounced on to the pavement.

"That's the wrong door," Chisa yelled from the checkout counter in the store.

Uruo picked a fallen broom and placed it gently with others that were standing.

"Don't worry about them things."

"Chisa, my cousin Hanbo is with me," Uruo said.

"Hi, Chisa," Hanbo said, bowing slightly.

"Hi." Chisa's dark face flushed all the way up to her ears.

"Hanbo's in high school."

"You guys are always welcome here. My mom watches the store every day."

"That's very nice." Hanbo glanced at her.

Chisa smiled at Hanbo and then turned to Uruo: "Come over here."

Jun-wan's face popped out from the pantry behind the counter. He came around and plunked down on a narrow floor space between the checkout counter and the threshold and then licked Uruo's leg.

"You know, Uruo, Jun-wan doesn't like people. He growls when customers come in so I have to keep him behind the counter. We don't want to lose our customers after all. He's usually in his doghouse in the backyard, though. I was surprised Jun-wan took to you at first sight. I couldn't believe it. I guess you smelled like a dog. What do you think?"

Uruo fired a high-pitched laugh at Chisa. "Grandma makes me take a bath every night. Hanbo goes first, then me and Grandma, and Aunt Kureo late at night."

Hanbo sat by Uruo and maintained his gaze on Chisa's expressive face.

"Why late at night?"

"She just—likes it that way, I guess." Hanbo's voice was low and gentle.

Jun-wan sat in front of Hanbo and sniffed his right knee.

"Antie Kureo makes sweaters."

"And sells them at the marketplace?"

Uruo nodded. "And our Grandma makes dried persimmons and takes them to the market, too."

"Yusa's Dried Persimmons?" Chisa leaned forward. "They are the best, let me tell you. My dad loves them. My mom buys four or five boxes at a time for him. At least she says they are for him. She seems to eat plenty on her own." Shrugging her shoulders, and covering her mouth with her hand, Chisa chuckled.

Chisa and Uruo stood up at the same time. She picked up Jun-wan's leash and handed it to Uruo. Jun-wan got up reluctantly.

Once outside, Chisa, Hanbo, Uruo, and Jun-wan had the east side of Namiki Street mostly to themselves. Only a few townspeople came toward them.

Uruo was aware of sidelong glances that some of the passersby cast at Chisa and him. As Hanbo and Chisa walked and talked together, Uruo hung back and studied Chisa's profile. The longer he looked, the more convinced Uruo was that she looked like a shiitake because of her bobbed hair, not so much because of her dark skin.

Jun-wan suddenly pulled Uruo forward. At the vine-covered tree across from Mr. Gen's bakery, he raised his right hind leg and relieved himself. Then Jun-wan sniffed the back of Uruo's hand, urging Uruo to stroke his head. Uruo scratched Jun-wan's neck.

They made a left at Mitsukaidō Station, turned right, and walked across the crossing southward to get to the other side of the station where street stalls stood side by side. By the staircase leading into the south entrance of the station was a red columnar mailbox that was about the same height as Chisa.

"There is the woman," Chisa shouted.

Jun-wan barked at Chisa.

"Who?" Hanbo asked.

"The sweet potato lady!" Chisa said, as if stating the obvious.

"Where?" Uruo was looking in the direction of where the street stalls were.

"Behind the mailbox," Hanbo said.

A woman in a kitchen apron, with a cloth over her head, sat behind a stone oven in a shape of a straw rice-bag. The oven was fastened to the bed of a large trailer with a single pair of bicycle wheels. The tin-plated chimney that jutted from the oven was sending up barely visible steam. The earthy sweet aroma of the roasted potatoes emanated from the oven.

The woman looked as though she was trying to see something in the invisible steam. Uruo stopped behind Hanbo and traced her blank stare, passing through the steam, all the way to the weather-beaten Jizō statue that stood at the entrance to the woods beyond the dirt road that ran in front of the street stalls. The woman's puzzling looks could mean she was praying for happiness, hoping to get her rich.

Uruo watched as Chisa gave the one-hundred-yen coin to the woman and heard her ask for six roasted sweet potatoes.

The woman opened the oven's round lid using a thick piece of rag. With a pair of bamboo tongs that were as long as her arm, she retrieved one potato and placed it in a paper bag made from old newspaper. Chisa asked to have three bags with two potatoes in each. The woman complied. The woman placed three bags on a narrow wooden counter away from the oven.

Uruo snatched a bag from the counter and dipped into it. "Ouch!" he screeched.

Chisa picked up a bag, rolled its top to close it, and passed it to Hanbo. "Be careful."

"Children, wait a while before you eat," the potato lady said. "You don't want to burn your mouths."

Chisa shot the woman a "don't-include-me-in-the-children" look. But the woman did not notice it, as she had already withdrawn into her meditation on the Jizō—perhaps until the next customer's arrival.

"Aren't we going to sit down and eat?" Uruo said.

"How about the other side of the station?" Hanbo said. "We can cross through inside."

The station's waiting room was nearly empty. The giant round clock on the wall above the ticket gate to the platform pointed to 1:20 in the afternoon. Uruo, Chisa, Hanbo sat on the bench long enough for three people.

"My potato's still hot," Uruo said, sucking in the air to cool a small piece he had bit off. Uruo mashed the potato in his mouth; and, pressing it between his tongue and the dome of his mouth, he sucked the sweetness out of it.

Chisa said nothing. She sat by the boys on the wooden bench, chiseling away at the steamy potato with her teeth.

Jun-wan, his front paws stretched out, sat in front of Chisa. His ears were straight up and twitching toward the gentle sucking noise Uruo was making, though neither Hanbo nor Chisa could hear it. Uruo threw him a smile, flashing his closed teeth. Jun-wan flattened his ears and wagged his tail, hitting the floor hard twice.

Suddenly Uruo gagged. The mashed sweet potato got stuck in his throat.

"What happened?" Chisa turned to Uruo. She instantly made her left hand into a fist and hit Uruo's upper back, increasing its intensity. Within a few seconds, a lump of mashed sweet potato popped out of Uruo's mouth and landed on the floor with a flat crushing noise. Jun-wan rushed to sniff it. Uruo sighed.

"You okay now?"

"Yeah." Uruo bent forward on the bench and held his forehead in his hands. Then he sat up and opened his bag and looked at Chisa first then Hanbo: "Any potatoes left?"

"I'm already on my second one," Hanbo said, his mouth full.

"I have one left still," Chisa said.

"Can I have it, Chisa?" Uruo's humble voice caught Hanbo's attention.

"Sure. But what are you going to do with it? Choke on it again?"

"No." Uruo took Chisa's bag. Sensing her bewilderment, Uruo walked over to the main entrance of the station and turned left toward the public toilet in the square.

Chisa and Hanbo stood up at the same time, dashed to the bench in front of the window. They jumped on it and glued their faces to the sooty windowpane at once.

Uruo stood about thirteen feet or so away from a man in khaki uniform, wrinkled and dirt stained. The man squatted, leaning against a wooden partition that separated the station square from the eastbound platform. Uruo tiptoed to the partition, his attention on the squatting man who had not noticed him. Uruo was unsure if the man was nodding or counting the coins scattered in a shallow tin box placed in front of him. Tracing the partition with his left hand and holding the two bags tightly in his right hand, Uruo stepped forward. He hesitated once again, biting his lower lip. His heartbeat echoed in his skull. At last he keeled by the man and offered him the two bags.

The man drew back, his eyes wide open, one of which pure white. The bags rustled as he squeezed them in his callused hands.

Uruo stood up. Chisa's and Hanbo's disapproving faces pierced Uruo's eyes. Shaken, Uruo turned around to look at the man.

Just then the man threw the bags into the trash box by the public toilet. "I don't want nothing from you, *kappa*. Go away!"

Jōji's voice clanged in Uruo's head. His hands clenched.

"Uruo! Don't!" Hanbo shouted.

Uruo stiffened.

Hanbo dashed out of the station building, grabbed at Uruo's arm, and pulled him back into the building. "Don't."

October 1960

"YOUR GREAT-GREAT granddad planted those persimmon trees, you know?"

"You've told me a thousand times, Grandma," Hanbo said, chuckling. "Maybe more."

Nao kept on peeling a large yellow persimmon, ignoring Hanbo. The small knife in her right hand glided over the fruit.

Hanbo picked up two persimmons from a pile in the basket by Nao and played with them as if they were a couple of beanbags.

"Leave them in the basket, Hanbo."

"They are heavier than they look."

"They are. I picked one hundred of them—all good and hard."

"When they ripen, crows will pick on them."

Nao shifted her legs on her floor cushion, letting her right leg dangle from the edge of the veranda. "You want to cut some strings for me, son?"

Hanbo picked up a roll of string and a pair of scissors that was lying by the basket.

"Take two fruits at a time and then …"

"Tie them with a piece of string at their stems, dip them in boiling water for five seconds, and hang them on the bamboo pole out there. Correct?"

With the tip of her tongue, Nao adjusted her denture on the lower left side—her habit she displayed when she was stuck on what to say.

"Do they sell good?"

"Oh, yes. I've known the manager there at the marketplace since he was younger than you are now. He puts a higher price on 'Yusa's Dried Persimmons' than he does on others. Such a kind boy."

Hanbo glanced at a portable clay stove placed on a stepping-stone outside the veranda. Water was boiling in a sooty pot.

Hanbo turned toward Uruo who was pushing his toy locomotive toward one of the persimmon trees. "Don't forget to up the signal—the train is arriving. Right?"

By the tree stood a toy traffic-light with a short horizontal wooden piece facing down. Uruo pushed the wooden piece up, to mean: "The train is coming. Be careful everyone." When Hanbo had made this traffic-light for Uruo, he used a screw and a bolt, instead of a nail, to fasten the two pieces together so that Uruo could move this short piece up and down easily.

Uruo returned right back to the well where he had left his train. The train was now approaching the imaginary station beyond the persimmon tree.

"Grandma."

Hanbo's voice, not often as low and serious as it was now, startled her. She stopped peeling the fruit. "What, son?"

Tying up a couple of persimmons with a string, and with his gaze fixed on her, Hanbo said: "I saw Master Kangen and Mrs. Kon visiting with you the other day." His gaze met hers.

"You've been thinking about it, haven't you?" Nao asked.

Hanbo hopped off the veranda, barefooted. He dipped a pair of fruits tied to the string into the boiling water and then slung the pair on the pole—the fruit on the left lower than the one on the right so that they wouldn't touch each other. "Are you sending him to Mitsukaidō Elementary?"

"You know the answer," Nao said as she picked up the half-peeled persimmon from the basket. "Parents don't want a dark boy with their kids. Master Kangen said they are afraid Uruo might cause more problems. The Tanges are the instigators, don't you know? A silly bunch of folks."

"I remember the fight." Hanbo chuckled as he jumped back up onto the veranda.

"Uruo's got a tough streak in him."

"You got it too, Grandma."

"He inherited it from his mother. You remember her—your Aunt Aoi?"

"Yeah. Before my father got transferred to Kagoshima. I was Uruo's age, I think."

"She was a strong-willed girl. The town's menfolk stayed away from her. No chance of any marriage there."

Hanbo cut more pieces of string out of the roll.

"Aoi left home five years after the Occupation began. There was no job for her here in Mitsukaidō. No job, no food. Only starvation."

"What happened to Grandpa's business? The Yusa Noodle Enterprise supplied most of the Imperial Army Bases in the Bōsō Peninsula, I heard."

"That's why the business got shot down. You look at giant conglomerates like Mitsubishi and Mitsui. They vanished under the Occupation because they had trade relations with the government. The Imperial Army was a major part of the government."

"And there's nothing left?"

"Not much. What money we had was all gone by 1950. Once she knew what was happening, Aoi packed her stuff in a large wrapping cloth and headed for Tokyo. She was twenty-one."

"Like a real soldier."

"A soldier? She was more of a man than those soldiers, I tell you. Soldiers receive orders. No one told her what to do. She was all on her own—in Tokyo, of all places."

"Did she write you at all?"

"Not for the first two months. Her first letter came from the Yokota U.S. Air Base in Tachikawa. She was working there as a blueprint drafter—the architectural planning unit of the base. She was the only woman, she wrote." Nao chuckled, with a mixed sense of pride and shame. "She enclosed two thousand yen."

"Gosh, that's a lot."

"She was a godsend, indeed." Nao sighed, put the peeled persimmon and the knife in the basket, pulled up her right leg that had been dangling from the veranda, and unfastened the two hooks that gathered her work pants at the ankle. She sat cross-legged on the cushion and picked up two unskinned persimmons, looked at them closely as if checking for blemishes, and squeezed them to see if they were hard enough for drying. "They are perfect," she mumbled.

The grating noise stopped and Kureo came out of her room. "I thought I heard you two." She stood by the pillar, looking down at her son and Nao sitting on the veranda.

"Why don't you join us? It's good to get some sunshine, Kureo."

"Help us with the persimmons, Mom."

"I've got some more work to do." Kureo pulled a floor cushion from the adjacent *tatami* room and sat down on it on her heels. "Aoi wasn't a godsend, you know."

"Oh, you heard what I said." Nao stopped peeling the yellow persimmon. "If she wasn't a godsend, then what was she?"

"I don't know." Kureo paused. "You made me marry when I was only eighteen. I begged you to let me go to school, like Aoi. But you didn't listen."

"It was good you married Lieutenant Doi. He was a fine man."

"I remember Dad," Hanbo said. "He was away most of the time, but when he was home he played with me. He was a soft spoken, gentle father."

"I wanted to teach grammar school. But I didn't have the education for it. But you ended up sending Aoi to a women's college."

"You had a husband from a prominent lineage. A strong will and intelligence were what Aoi had—not that you didn't have all these things. I just never thought she was a marrying type to begin with. That's the reason I sent her to college. So that she could be certified to become a professional in some field."

"Aoi ended up disgracing our family—she slept with a black man of foreign origin and then had his kid. I don't approve of it, and I don't accept Uruo as my nephew either—he is of black blood. Foreign, American blood. Uruo is a son of a man from the country that murdered my husband in the war. I shall never forget it." Kureo abruptly covered her mouth, stood up, and dashed back into her room. The sliding screen slammed shut. Wailing followed.

"Let me go see her," Hanbo said.

"Leave her alone. She'll get over it. She must learn to let go of the past." Nao's knife reflected the sun over the yellow persimmon.

"Fine. Where is Tachikawa, by the way?" Hanbo asked.

"West of Tokyo."

"You've been there?"

"Once, in 1955."

"Uruo was already born then? Why did you go there?"

"For important business. You don't need to know it, Hanbo. At least for now." Nao's gentle gaze suddenly turned stern. Hanbo's curiosity was stirred even more.

The sound of the boiling water on the clay stove stood out in the abrupt silence. It swelled aloud, separating Nao and Hanbo like an invisible stone wall so thick that nothing could smash it. Then the noise subsided.

"When Uruo was born, the Korean War was still going on," Nao muttered to herself. "He was born here, in this house. Just as you were."

"You never talk about Uruo's dad."

"There isn't much to tell you, son."

"What do you mean, Grandma?"

"Well, I can only tell you what Aoi had told me."

Hanbo put a pair of tied persimmons in front of his crossed legs.

"His name was Bob something. Was it Dickinson, or Denison, maybe it was Dixon … I don't remember. Anyway, in time, they got to know each other well because they were working in the same work unit. He was a designer engineer based in the Yokota U.S. Air Base in Tachikawa, not a soldier. Soon Bob rented a house outside the base—in those days, high ranking officers and personnel could live outside the base. Aoi had said some of them even bought houses. She moved in with Bob. They were married as far as they were concerned. But … it was not like your parents' marriage. Soon

Aoi got pregnant with Uruo—she was twenty-three. The Korean War was still going on. Bob was reassigned to Korea on emergency notice, and Aoi lost the house because the house was under Bob's name. But she could rent a small room in an apartment complex inside the base where many non-military personnel lived, she said. It was about this time she started to come home on weekends. I was so happy to have her back home, even for a few days a week.

"The base gave her maternity leave, without pay. She took three weeks off after Uruo was born. I became Uruo's nanny. It was perfectly fine with me—I'm his grandmother after all.

"One day she complained about severe cough, chest pain, and loss of voice. Then she started taking sick days, with no pay. She was exhausted. Got so thin. Three months later, she passed away. She was twenty-seven.

"Uruo thinks his mother is still in Lotus Land and is coming back soon. When Aoi was home, Uruo never left her side. They had a special bond. She always brought him presents—candy, toys, clothes, American books he could not read. That yellow train he is playing with over there? She bought it for him at the base. It's a good one, made in America."

"What happened to Uruo's dad?"

Grandma Nao stopped her hands once again and looked at Uruo who were pushing his yellow train back and forth on the imaginary railroad track between the well and the persimmon tree. "Aoi never mentioned his name once he was gone to Korea. I do remember the war ended in 1953. I imagine he returned to America—to his real family. Or he was killed in action. Nobody knows."

"Was Aunt Aoi his *only-san*?"

A volcanic shock landed on the left side of Hanbo's face. He fell on the veranda floor from the force of his grandmother's slap.

"Don't you dare say that word again, Hanbo! Aoi was never a leech. She was a U.S. employee. She earned her living just as he did. She sent me two thousand yen every month, and half of it went to you and your mother when you were living in Kagoshima. Have you forgotten that? What a filthy thing to say."

"I'm so sorry, Grandma."

"Do you even know what the word means? It means a high-class whore who pretends to be a soldier's wife while he stations in this country. Who serves him just so that she can go to America with him when he goes back home."

Hanbo shuddered at the thought of imagining Uruo's mother this way. He did not know whose forgiveness he should seek. "I didn't know. I didn't."

"You won't do it again, will you?" The knife in her hand continued to make a hissing noise like a crawling snake as it peeled a greenish persimmon.

"No, Grandma, I won't."

"Now, go to the well and cool your face in water. I know it hurt."

Hanbo slipped his feet into his *geta* with tattered black thongs.

Nao's gaze, at once embracing and spurning, followed him to the well. "Aoi named that boy," recalled Nao. "If he could call her an '*only-san*,' could he have also resented his cousin because he was born of a citizen of the country who killed his father in the war?"

Nao let this thought play in her head as she sliced at the persimmons, cutting each one with more force than the last.

October 1959

CHISA CAME out of the kitchen. Nao followed and stood by her. They said nothing.

Hanbo's and Uruo's faces turned blank.

"It's Jun-wan," Nao said.

"Where is Jun-wan?" Uruo frowned.

"He's in the animal hospital. My dad is with him." Chisa's voice faltered. "He wanted me to tell you."

"Go with Chisa, son. The hospital isn't far."

Chisa grabbed Uruo's arm. At the same time her pupils expanded, and her lips parted at the sight of Hanbo who was standing among the flock of hens. Hanbo stared at her perfectly oval dark face, fascinated by faint curvatures across her chest.

"You coming?" Uruo threw a quizzical gaze.

"No." Hanbo bent over and cleaned the bucket that was already empty. He raised his eyes when Chisa and Uruo made a left toward the gate.

A nurse came out to the foyer of the animal hospital to greet Chisa and Uruo. The nurse stood there, agape at these dark-skinned children.

"My dad is here with our dog. I am his daughter, Chisa. And this is my younger brother, Uruo."

"I am—" Uruo shut right up, sensing Chisa made up this sibling relationship to protect him.

The nurse stared at them, her hand across her mouth. Her stare shifted to Uruo.

"Our ancestors are from the South Pacific: That's what my grandfather used to tell me. Now, can we go in to see the rest of our family?"

"Why—, of course. Please follow me." The nurse led the way into the room where Jun-wan lay on the operating table. The nurse's stare carved itself into Uruo's memory.

A brief sob escaped through Chisa's lips. She dabbed her eyes and cleared her throat.

Uruo stood by the operating table, sandwiched by a veterinarian in a white surgical coat and Chisa's father, whose face was as dark as hers. Mr. Suda glanced at Uruo and nodded as he paid attention to the vet explaining what was happening to Jun-wan. The odor of cresol, which filled the room, felt like it could suffocate him.

On the stainless table Jun-wan lay on his side. His left leg seemed shorter than his right. Perhaps he lost part of his left leg when he was hit by a truck. Thick layers of blood-stained bandages protected a wound extending around his trunk. His front paw stretched flaccid. His hollow eyes stared into space.

"May I touch him?" Uruo whispered to the vet.

"Very gently."

Uruo touched Jun-wan's forehead. Jun-wan's ears flattened and his tail stroked the table surface once. Uruo brought his nose near Jun-wan's muzzle. Jun-wan gave Uruo a gentle lick that hardly touched Uruo's nose. A high-pitched noise, like wind pushing itself through a tiny hole on the wall, escaped from Jun-wan's muzzle.

Chisa and her father were watching over Uruo and Jun-wan. Chisa embraced Uruo from behind, her arms across his chest, guarding him from shock.

"Jun-wan's going to be all right?"

"I hope so," Mr. Suda murmured.

Three days later, about noon, Uruo walked over to the trapezoidal stone to wait for Chisa. The stone was warm, as if the sun had heated it for Uruo to sit in comfort. Since he had touched the wounded Jun-wan at the animal hospital, Uruo had been thinking how beautiful it would be to have a big dog like Jun-wan. Nao did not think their backyard had enough acreage for a big dog to run around. She did not say that Uruo could not have a dog, but that he should think how the dog would feel having to live in a small space. Uruo knew the answer.

Chisa opened the sliding door of her general store across the street and came out, holding in her arms a small box that was wrapped in a cloth striped in pale blue and white, its four corners tied on top. Uruo's gaze riveted on that box as Chisa crossed Namiki Street.

"Ready?" Chisa said.

"Where to?"

"The forest." Chisa paused. "Jun-wan didn't make it. He lost too much blood—that's what Dad said."

"Where is Jun-wan now?"

"Right here."

"In the box?"

"The vet did it for us." Chisa stroked the back of Uruo's head where soft curls had grown thick. "Jun-wan became flames and soared into the sky."

Uruo looked up into the spotless autumn sky. He extended his hands to Chisa and she placed the box gently in them. Uruo held the box against his chest while walking, until they stood in front of the closed crossing. The red light was blinking, accompanied by the warning bell. The railroad tracks trembled. Chisa stepped away, touched Uruo's arm and led him back from the crossing. With its wheels crashing against the tracks, the steam engine blew past them like a gigantic black wind and disappeared into the valley west of the town. The crossing opened, and the warning bell stopped.

A narrow dirt road stretched parallel to the forest line. Chisa and Uruo passed the stone Jizō with a red cloth napkin across his chest. Uruo followed Chisa, wondering if the sweet potato lady might have put the napkin on the Jizō.

Uruo stopped and gazed at the Jizō under a canopy of colored foliage that blocked off the sun. The forest seemed still as midnight—filled with a darkness that could encircle and swallow the whole world until he would never see the light of the day again. A cold sensation pricked his back, like millions of burning needles. The darkness of the forest suddenly seemed menacing.

Uruo held the box as tight as he could and ran straight on the dirt road.

"This is the spot." Chisa made a right at an oval lot where more than two dozen weather-beaten stumps lay scattered among weeds—a reservoir of sunshine in the middle of the dark forest.

"See the spruce tree there at the far corner?"

"I like it." Uruo spoke for the first time since they had past the crossing. "Chisa." Uruo handed the box back to her.

Dead leaves had filled around the tree and had created a thick cushion surrounding the exposed rugged roots. Chisa and Uruo walked around the spruce tree, first clockwise then counterclockwise before they found an open space where two largest roots forked outward. Chisa swept a heap of leaves there with her foot until the dark soil peeked out. Uruo, on his knees, raked the rest of the leaves with his hands. He then dug the soil with a piece of triangular flat stone about eight inches long. But the soil was soft, so Uruo discarded the flat stone and used his hands to dig. He made a hole the size of the wooden pail that Nao kept by the well. Uruo got up and nodded to Chisa, who was sitting on a stump with the box on her lap, gazing blankly at the flat stone Uruo had discarded.

Chisa knelt and placed the box gently in the hole. Uruo watched her return the soil back into the hole and cover it with the leaves that Uruo had raked. She remained motionless. She sobbed, silently.

Uruo looked into the deep blue sky and said to himself: "Junwan's in the Land of Lotus. My Mama is up there, too."

⁓

The faded *shōji* slid open. The early afternoon sun gushed into the six-*tatami* room. Uruo turned to the sudden brightness and squinted.

"Help me, Uruo. I have two pine branches," Nao whispered as she came in. She gave him one of the branches.

Nao's *tabi* was white. Her *kimono* and *haori* were black with no creases. She had her salt-and-pepper hair styled in a high bun: it shone in dark silver. She brought in the aroma of mothballs with her.

He scrutinized Nao's new looks from her head to toe.

Nao sat down in front of the alcove, by him, and patted his right cheek as she had always done. "Hold on to this for me, Uruo."

He took a tree branch from her. "It's got a funny smell, Grandma."

"Remember the *kadomatsu* we put outside the house, to celebrate New Year's Day?"

"Um."

"The bush holding three bamboo pieces together?"

"Yes."

Nao caressed the tip of pine needles with her palm. "These are the same kind."

Uruo patted his branch needles with his palm. The needles resisted and poked him. He pressured them more. The needles responded giving more pain into his palm.

"Hurts, doesn't it?" Nao smiled at him. "Better keep your hand away from the needles." She then gave out a short but loud grunt and stuck her pine branch right into the frog in the water in a round flat vase. The vase had a forked crack on its surface. Uruo thought the water might seep out through the crack; this thought startled him.

"Let me have your branch, Uruo." With a pair of pruning shears, she trimmed off the tip of the branch diagonally and placed the other end into the vase. She trimmed the branch and pressed it hard into the frog. Uruo's eyes brightened when he saw two pine branches together in the vase, the slanted one half-encircling the other, filling the space between the vase and the calligraphic scroll above. It looked like two little people talking to each other, the scroll's last character listening in on them.

"Come with me." Nao stood up and extended her left hand. In her black creaseless *kimono* and white *tabi*, she appeared suddenly taller. When he took her hand, the smell of mothballs from her *kimono* made him sneeze. But his sneezing stopped when his eyes caught a long wooden box laying in front of the closed sliding-screens, which he had not noticed before when he came into the room.

Uruo paused.

"What?"

Uruo looked up at Nao and then turned to the wooden box.

"Don't you want to see your Mama?"

He nodded.

Aoi had been in and out of her *futon* for some time, always coughing and breathing hard. A mixed stench of excrement, urine, and sweat had pervaded the room and had never seemed to go away. Nao stayed by Aoi, rubbing her colorless feet and haggard hands, massaging her neck and shoulders. Aoi had hardly spoken to anyone, except when Nao brought Uruo to her. With her emaciated arms, she would push herself up so that she could sit up on her *futon* and put on a robe. She would then extend her hands and mutter to Uruo, "My son." Uruo would sit on Aoi's lap and cling to her shoulder, immersing himself in her warm body odor. Holding her son, she would rock back and forth, not saying a word to him. He knew her warmth belonged to no one, only to him.

Uruo let Nao take him to the wooden box. She gently guided him by his shoulder. They sat by the wooden box. She then touched the lid of the box. After a pause, she opened the lid and let it slide down between the long side of the box and the sliding screens.

"Mama," Uruo whispered into the box. "Is she okay?"

From the family altar set on a chest in the other room, the scent of incense drifted into the six-*tatami* room. It reminded Uruo of the tombstones clustered along the ginkgo trees on the way to the temple school.

"Yes. She is resting. She has a long journey ahead of her."

"A journey?"

"Yes. To the Land of Lotus where orchids are in full bloom all year long."

"Mama." Uruo touched Aoi's white hands clasped across her chest. Her hands were cold despite the bright sun casting its warmth into the room. Uruo turned to Nao. "Can I stay by Mama?"

"No. Not this time."

"Why can't I?"

"She is all cleaned up to meet the Great One in Paradise." Nao pulled him close to her and held him.

Uruo could see Aoi's feet and the hem of her *kimono*. Like Nao, Aoi wore a pair of white *tabi*. Some rose petals scattered about the hem of her white *kimono*.

"Is that a nice place, Grandma?"

"Yes. If you are a good boy, you can go there to be with your Mama, aunts and uncles, great-grandparents, and many more."

Uruo gazed at Aoi, resting his chin on his hands as he grasped the edge of the wooden box, wondering why his mother was cold.

Nao lifted the lid and inlaid it into the wooden box.

The sliding-screens slowly opened into the dark main room. There the guests sat in rows and joined their hands in prayer.

Nao pushed Uruo toward the veranda, whispering for him to go outside and play.

November 1959

THE HOUSE was dark. Nobody had yet opened the sliding shutters that enclosed the veranda on the west and south sides. Uruo, half-awake under his *futon* spread on the *tatami* floor of the alcove room, heard the squeaking of the hand pump at the well followed by the noise of water hitting the bottom of the wooden bathtub. The noise traveled like the ebb and flow of the tide. Uruo leaned to his right: Hanbo's *futon* remained on tatami, empty and untidy. To his left was Nao's *futon*, folded in three, ready to be put away into the bedding closet by the alcove. This is how he slept—flanked by Nao and Hanbo. Aunt Kureo rarely left her four-*tatami* room, where she spent long nights working. In the warmth of *futon*, Uruo felt shielded. He was content.

The noise from the well subsided. The smell of rice, boiling in the cauldron in the kitchen, drifted to fill the house. Uruo tasted the aroma. The sweet smell of rice meant *osekihan*. Nao cooked *osekihan* on festive days such as Children's Festival in May and Lantern Festival in August. A mixture of sticky rice, red beans, and salt and sesame seed sprinkled over it made Uruo salivate—it was his favorite food, though he could only enjoy it on special occasions. Food was always scarce, and Uruo understood. Otherwise, Nao would not visit Gen's bakery once a week to receive free bread crusts. The image of Nao holding a brown bagful of bread crusts and bowing to show her gratitude to Gen—it was loudly painted on his mental canvas.

Much as Uruo was happy to have *osekihan*, he did not grasp why Nao had cooked this special dish when it was not a festive day. He questioned if today's train trip to Tokyo would be something special? Uruo's curiosity only intensified.

Nao had promised him this trip long ago. Even if Nao had not promised, he would have gone to Tokyo on his own when he had grown up. He toyed with the idea of going to Tokyo with Hanbo when he graduated high school and obtained a job in the city. But this idea sounded too much like a dream he could not capture. Too complicated for him to handle for now. Besides, he did not want to burden Hanbo in any way.

But a surge of excitement kept radiating deep inside his skull. He would have a lot to tell Chisa about today's trip when he got back from Tokyo this evening.

The sliding shutters at the veranda grated on the wooden rail; and, one by one, they settled into a narrow shutter case attached to the outer wall of Aunt Kureo's room. The *shōji* partitions that stood between the veranda and the six-*tatami* room brightened. The sun cast its autumnal warmth.

"Hey, wake up," Hanbo yelled from outside as he pushed the last shutter into the case. "Grandma's waiting for you."

"Smells good."

"It's not done yet. Go take a bath with Grandma." Hanbo drummed the veranda floor with his hands, fast and loud, to annoy Uruo. He kicked his *geta* off, hopped onto the veranda, and opened the *shōji* partitions. Uruo was still under the *futon*. Hanbo tore off Uruo's *futon,* laughing. "Up, up, up. Go pee, then to the bath hut."

"Don't," Uruo yelled at Hanbo, grabbed Hanbo's unmade *futon* on the right, and covered himself from head to toe with it.

"Come on." Hanbo peeled the *futon* from Uruo again and threw a *yukata* at him. Uruo crumpled the *yukata* into a ball and threw it back at Hanbo and got up and ran to the toilet at the south end of the veranda.

Passing by the family altar in the eight-*tatami* room, Hanbo entered the kitchen where the *osekihan* was frothing in the cauldron, pushing up the lid.

⁓

At Mitsukaidō Station, Uruo leaned against a rusted iron support on the platform. Nao and Hanbo sat in the old wooden bench with faded varnish.

"Have some of these." Hanbo opened a basket filled with jelly beans, blue, white, and yellow—a gift from Nao to Uruo.

"I want lots of yellows." Uruo cupped his hands. Hanbo dropped one jelly bean at a time into Uruo's palms, and Uruo counted aloud. His limpid voice echoed in the fresh late morning air of the empty platform.

"Faster, Hanbo."

"You got enough for now." Hanbo picked up two pieces from the basket. And he tossed one up in the air and swiftly brought his mouth underneath to catch it. "Can you do it?"

Uruo looked at the jelly beans in his left hand, picked up a blue one, and placed it on his tongue. "I don't want to drop it."

"Smart boy," muttered Nao and tee-heed at Hanbo.

A penetrating pitch warbled. A kite circled over the forest, surveying the world below. The kite dove into the forest. Then, with its pray gripped in its claws, the kite hurtled into the sky and flew away.

Uruo sat by Nao and crammed four jelly beans into his mouth. Nao was listening to the steam engine arriving from east. She stood up. Hanbo handed Uruo the jelly bean basket.

"I'll be back tonight, Hanbo." Uruo looked at Hanbo who, in turn, touched Uruo's soft amber cheek.

"It's here." The steam engine overpowered Nao's whisper.

Uruo and Nao were the only passengers who got on the train.

The steam engine whistled loud and slid out of Mitsukaidō Station.

By the old bench, Hanbo watched the train follow the curve of the tracks into the valley between two mountain ridges.

⁓

Two hours later, Nao and Uruo got off the train. The train station signboard read "Chinosaki." A thick layer of gravel covered a small plaza in front of the station. A two-story eatery, a grocery store, a gift shop, a taxi pick-up area, and a bus terminal spacious enough for two buses made up the plaza. On the left side of the eatery extended a concrete road sloping down toward Highway 256 that ran along the Pacific seacoast toward the southwest. To the right side of the station, across the plaza, stretched a long stone wall about ten feet high, upon which spread a panorama of colored foliage and evergreen trees all mixed to amass a hilly estate. Attached to the stone walls on both sides, a sturdy iron gate opened outward. Beyond that, a pebbled path shone white, bending rightward, enclosed by meticulously spaced young pine trees.

"Are you hungry?"

"Yes, Grandma. I see a place over there." Uruo pointed at the two-story eatery with his finger.

"What are you hungry for?"

"Maybe *osekihan*—like this morning?"

"They don't have it, son." Nao took Uruo's hand. "Let's go in and see what they have."

The gravel echoed their footsteps in irregular rhythm.

"Anybody here?" Nao and Uruo went in and chose a table near the entrance. Uruo handed his basket to Nao, which she placed by her.

A thin middle-aged woman came out to take orders, apologizing for not tending the eatery. Nao's smile told her: "We are in no hurry." Nao bowed. She ordered two rice cakes with sweet bean jam inside and a cup of green tea. And she looked at Uruo. He pointed at a small picture of ice cream with a strawberry on top of it posted on the wall across his table.

"Orange juice for you, too?" The woman jotted down their orders. "Are you from St. Veronica's?"

"No. We are visiting the place," Nao said.

"More kids are arriving these days, I hear."

Nao nodded. Outside the window, autumn leaves swirled quietly.

The waitress put the checkbook in her apron pocket and disappeared behind the counter. When she returned with their orders, she had a small piece of angel cake with the vanilla ice cream.

"Is that for him?"

"My treat." She served Nao first.

"I'm grateful," Nao said with her eyes downcast.

"Not at all." The waitress watched Uruo taste his first spoonful of ice cream. "Do you like it?"

"It's so good, ma'am."

The waitress patted Uruo's back and smoothed creases on his new white sweater. "I am glad."

The wind had picked up. Nao and Uruo walked on the pavement along the stone wall toward the iron gate. Uruo jumped and hopped to catch floating leaves and put them in his basket which was still half filled with jelly beans.

Inside the iron gate, to the right of the pebbled path, laid an enormous gray boulder, rugged in its shape. Mounted on it was a patinated copper plaque: ST. VERONICA'S HOME FOR CHILDREN.

In the reception room of St. Veronica's Home sat Sister Ōgin, Father Sainen, Nao, and Uruo. Nao spoke quietly, her eyes downcast on a large brown growth ring on the mahogany table. Nao spoke to Father Sainen, then to Sister Ōgin, the Home's executive director. Father Sainen listened to Nao, his body thrust forward, nodding. Sister Ōgin's permed short black hair exposed her large octagonal face. Uruo had never seen a woman with her back perfectly straight, parallel to the back of the chair she was sitting in. She drew her chin in, which pushed her breasts out far. A fluffy white jabot rested on her large breasts. Uruo trembled at her piercing sidelong glare.

Although he did not grasp most of what those grown-ups were discussing, Uruo did catch Sister Ōgin declaring that, once a child was placed under St. Veronica's care, no family members could be allowed to see him until the child turned fifteen years of age. This was St. Veronica's strict code, and the family must abide by it. Uruo quailed before Sister Ōgin. He joined his hands between his knees under the mahogany table, dropping his eyes on his running shoes. He sensed he would not see Nao and Hanbo for a long time. Beads of sweat covered his forehead, and his chest quivered.

Nao stood up and bowed to Sister Ōgin and Father Sainen. Nao put on her *geta* in the vestibule off the reception room. She said nothing, and she did not look back as she left the building.

Uruo stood inside the vestibule. "Grandma ..."

Her dark formal kimono was becoming smaller by the second, and the sound of her *geta* accelerated on the pebbled long path.

"Grandma!" Uruo dashed out of the vestibule after her.

Barefooted, Sister Ōgin ran out, chasing after Uruo. Sister Ōgin pulled up her plain black skirt above the knee, her ruffled jabot bouncing left and right across her chest. "Get back in here, Uruo Yusa!" She caught up with Uruo within seconds. She grabbed his arm and twirled him around to face her and slapped him in the face. Another crushing blow on the right cheek sent Uruo into a globe-shaped holly bush that grew parallel to the Home's main office building. Uruo's face stuck in the bush.

Father Sainen, who had followed Sister Ōgin from the reception room, leaned into the bush, and took Uruo up in his arms. A thick red stream ran down from Uruo's left temple and dripped onto his shoulder, staining his white sweater bright red. Father Sainen kneeled, held Uruo, gently patted his trembling back. It did not help ease his bawling.

"Let the nurse take care of him," Sister Ōgin commanded. She looked down her nose at Uruo, her hands on her hips. As if nothing had happened, she returned to the office building where an office staff gave her a wet rag to wipe her bare feet clean.

Uruo fought against Father Sainen's strong embrace: He wanted to catch up with Nao, who had not looked back and was now about to make a right turn toward the iron gate.

"Grandma, take me home!" Uruo shouted.

Nao kept walking as if she did not hear her grandson, as if he were not hers. Then, she was no longer there.

PART 02

Chinosaki

1959 ~ 1967

November 1959

URUO'S WAILING let up into sobs. Father Sainen remained undaunted by Uruo's mood change. Father Sainen had gone through it with most of the sixty-seven children who had become the residents of this welfare institution. With some exceptions, the children went through three phases: resistance, resignation, and acceptance. Some children had continued to resist longer than expected.

"Don't you want to meet your brothers and sisters?" Father Sainen examined Uruo's wound on the left temple. "Still bleeding. We'd better go to the nurse's office first."

"Brothers" and "sisters"—Cousin Hanbo was the only "brother" he had known.

Annexed to the east side of the office building was a nurse's office with a pair of sliding glass windows.

The entrance door opened. "Good afternoon, Father Sainen and ...?" The nurse's face was perfectly round, defined by the front curvature of her nurse's cap across her forehead.

"Mrs. Mori, this is Uruo Yusa. He arrived today."

"Come in, both of you."

Uruo ascended three long and shallow stone steps, took off his shoes at the tiled foyer, and entered the office. Father Sainen kept his hand on Uruo's back so that he would not run away. Mrs. Mori closed the door after the priest and suggested that Uruo put on a pair of slippers at the foyer.

The smell of iodine caged Uruo motionless. It stirred the jelly beans still left in his stomach. He trembled at the possibility that they might tie him up on the table.

The sliding window was open. But a fine light green net protected the window from outside, which made the bushes, the pine trees, and the buildings outside appeared grayer than how they would look under the direct sun.

Six large panels comprised the ceiling, each the size of a *tatami.* Finely shredded wooden pieces congealed into square panels. Painted white, these shreds overlapped and intertwined in chaos, as if they were in perpetual motion. No cracks could be found.

"Now, this will sting a little." Mrs. Mori's round face blocked the ceiling from Uruo's sight. With a wet gauze, she gently wiped the coagulated blood about his left temple, across his cheek, and along his neck. After she had repeated this routine with a clean gauze, she medicated his temple with a yellow ointment and covered it with a wide bandage. Because of the strange characters printed on top of the bandage box, Uruo recognized it came from America. These characters resembled the book his mother had brought home a long ago—the book with the blond girl on its front cover.

Mrs. Mori traced Uruo's gaze to the Band-Aid box. "Do you read English? Did you speak it with your dad?"

"No, ma'am."

"Uruo lived with his grandmother, a cousin, and his aunt," Father Sainen said.

"I see. Well, you'll have one big family here." Mrs. Mori gently ruffled Uruo's curly hair. "You wait here, I'll get a clean shirt for you."

When she returned, she unbuttoned Uruo's bloody shirt and cleaned up his blood-stained left shoulder and arm with a large pad soaked with alcohol. A ray of tenderness shone in her eyes as she handed him a clean short sleeve. He wanted to hug her and let it all out. Instead, he maintained his composure: Sister Ōgin's punishment was much too vivid a memory to open himself to anyone in this new place.

Father Sainen bowed his gratitude to Mrs. Mori. Then he and Uruo headed for the playground that spread behind the three-story dormitory attached to west of the main office building.

That night, Miss Hogi, the house mother assigned to the children grouped on the third floor of the dormitory, told Uruo to sleep in an empty railed bed sitting at the entrance to this room. The beds lined up in rows on both sides of a narrow aisle. This room was only for sleeping, Miss Hogi explained to Uruo. The children did everything else in the ten-*tatami* room next to the bedroom. For breakfast and dinner, this ten-*tatami* room transformed into an eatery: The children rolled in three round tables that were all short-legged and foldable and each could seat five children. When children returned from the school building, the space turned into an all-purpose room. Some children did their homework, and others read. Several of them congregated in a corner of the room to play with a large picture puzzle donated by the American Red Cross.

"Oh, there's the puzzle back there." Uruo pointed to the unfinished puzzle spread out at the corner. "May I play with it?"

"Yes, when you've come back from school tomorrow."

"Am I going to school?"

"Yes, of course."

"I don't want to."

"May I ask why?"

"They will call me 'Coal Boy,' ma'am."

"Here at St. Veronica's, no one will call you that name."

The children slowly gathered in the center of the room on the *tatami* floor and sit properly in circle.

"Let's join them." Miss Hogi sat, with Uruo by her.

The evening prayer began with a song Uruo had never heard of. Next everyone cited a prayer in unison: "Our Father who art in heaven ..." Afterwards, a girl recited her own prayer, which was really a report on what she had done that day. Uruo's feet were going numb, but he endured the discomfort: Nobody else showed any sign of pains and aches. The prayer ended with another song similar to the one they had sung earlier. Miss Hogi said, "Good night everybody." And the children responded in unison: "Good night, Miss Hogi." All got up and headed for the bedroom, chatting and giggling with one another.

Miss Hogi handed Uruo clean pajamas. He unfolded them. The pajamas had shoulders, arms, middle, and legs all in one piece. "Ma'am, I don't know how to put it on." Anticipating hard slaps across his face, he covered his head with his arms, dropping the pajamas on the *tatami* floor.

"It's all right. Nothing to worry about." Miss Hogi picked up and unbuttoned the pajamas. Then she instructed him to remove his shirt and trousers and slip into the pajamas, his feet first.

Uruo liked the pajamas: a cocoon would be like this. "Thank you, ma'am."

Miss Hogi smiled and cupped Uruo's face with her hands. Looking into his almond-shaped hazel eyes, she said, "You'll do fine—I know it."

The blanket itched, and it took a few minutes to get warm under it. Uruo missed his *futon* at home. He missed the comfort and security of sleeping between Nao and Cousin Hanbo. He yearned for the old six-*tatami* room with its slight aroma of sourness. That was his home. He was supposed to have returned home by the evening. Nao walking alone with a white handkerchief across her mouth, the noise pebbles made after her footsteps, the pine trees swaying as if ushering her out of the Home, the insult, the rage, the fear that Sister Ōgin's punishment evoked—these fragments kept racing through his brain. None of them made sense to him.

The night light at the end of the aisle illuminated the chaotic patterns of the ceiling. With his numbed imagination, Uruo was staring at the ceiling patterns when he heard a whisper. It was coming from the bed next to him.

"Hi, Uruo."

"How do you know my name?" Uruo did not move.

"Everybody knows everybody else."

"I don't know you."

"I'm Marendo. They call me 'Marendo' so it must be my name." He tittered.

Uruo chuckled and turned to Marendo, his blanket up to his chin.

"Let's go to school together, tomorrow."

Through the reflection of the night light, Uruo could see Marendo's socketed eyes; his long straight hair with a dull shine to it; and his high-bridged straight nose.

"Okay," Uruo whispered back. Fascinated, Uruo focused on Marendo's profile in silhouette.

April 1961

THE CHILDREN called them "hello-*san*." Their visitations to St. Veronica's Home continued—sometimes alone, other times in groups. They always greeted the children with "Hello."

Hello-*san* were not from where Uruo was born and raised: Their words were different, and their voices gentle and smooth. When they spoke to the children, they squatted down to the children's heights. And they spoke as if these American-looking children could comprehend their words while the children could speak only Japanese. While the children were required to take English two hours a week at school, learning the language was not the same as being able to speak it. Sister Ōgin and Father Sainen gave the hello-*san* the tour of the Home. And they interpreted for the children. Still, the children viewed the hello-*san* as strangers who spoke a different language, who dressed in light khaki uniforms that fit them perfectly. There were light skinned hello-*san*, like Marendo; then there were dark hello-*san*. Uruo favored dark hello-*san* because they reminded him of a man whom he used to call "Dad" when he was a small boy. A dark hello-*san* had visited St. Veronica's last month. Uruo had cherished his memory since.

That afternoon, the hello-*san* was with Father Sainen. Uruo was playing catch with Marendo in the playground. Despite his age, Uruo had broad shoulders and thick arms which gave him pitching power and extra speed. Marendo was taller but thinner. His pitch was smooth and controlled. So far Marendo had caught all of Uruo's pitches. But his canvas glove was getting ripped at the connective point between the thumb and the forefinger which he called "the web." Uruo kept pitching at him. Suddenly Marendo dodged, letting the baseball fly and then bounce a few times toward the net that separated the playground from a hilly pine wood beyond.

"Your glove?"

"It's done for."

"You know what?" Uruo was proud that he knew something Marendo presumably did not. "Let's go see the laundry lady."

"Which one? Granny Shizu?"

"Yeah. She made these gloves." Uruo exchanged his cotton-filled canvas glove with Marendo's flattened glove with the filler cotton sticking out of the rip. "Granny Shizu can fix it for us."

"Now?"

"Why not? She should be in the laundry room."

"What if she is too busy?"

"Let's ask her first."

The two boys passed by the crape myrtle growing in front of Sister Ōgin's suite and headed for the laundry room. Uruo kept undoing the thick black thread that Granny Shizu had used to stich up the outer rim of the glove.

"Let Granny do it," Marendo said.

"If all the threads are pulled out, all she has to do is stuff the canvas with more cotton and machine-sew it."

"Okay."

"Boys, could you come here for a minute?" It was Father Sainen. By the decorative garden stone about six feet high and as thick as an ancient Roman pillar that sat imposingly across from Sister Ōgin's suite a distance away, Father Sainen stood with a dark hello-*san*.

Uruo and Marendo paused.

"Yes, you two there." Father Sainen drew large circles in the air with his hand, urging the boys to come faster.

Marendo stayed behind Uruo. The hello-*san* was so tall that next to him Uruo looked like a cicada perched on the chinquapin tree that grew by the boys' dormitory newly built on the estate's hilltop. Marendo gave a faint smile.

The man said hello to Uruo, offering him a rugged hand that was at least three times larger than Uruo's.

Father Sainen's eyes encouraged Uruo to respond.

Uruo nodded, shifted his gaze from Father Sainen to the hello-*san*, and took the hello-*san*'s hand precariously. Uruo could hold only a half of the hello-*san*'s hand. Keeping Uruo's hand in his, and beaming, the hello-*san* said something to Uruo, which Uruo did not catch. This was Uruo's first one-on-one encounter with a person who spoke to him in a language that was different from his. Uruo's heartbeat accelerated. Father Sainen at once interpreted for Uruo the hello-*san*'s questions, and Uruo answered them all: He said in English that he was nine years old, and that he enjoyed school. But, unable to talk about his future dream, he turned to Father Sainen and said in Japanese that he wanted to become a conductor of locomotives, which Father Sainen interpreted to the hello-*san*. While talking, the hello-*san* pulled Uruo close to him and put his arm around his shoulder. As their conversation went on, the hello-*san* pointed to the ripped glove that Uruo held under his arm. Uruo showed him the ripped glove and said in strained English: "I am good pitcher"; and gestured to pitch. The hello-*san* nodded his understanding and extended his hand. Uruo put the glove on his palm. The hello-*san* examined the glove, tracing the stitches with his fingers—impressed by the way it was put together with a piece of canvas. Then he pulled out some of the cotton filler, surprised that a baseball glove could be made this way—with a piece of canvas, cotton, and durable thread.

The hello-*san* and Father Sainen engaged in a private conversation. Uruo was no longer the center of their attention. He turned around to see what Marendo was doing. Marendo showed Uruo the glove he had and stuck out his chin to signal for him to get the ripped glove back from the hello-*san*. Uruo pulled the hello-*san*'s starched light khaki shirt that was fastened at the wrist, pointed the ripped glove still held in his huge hand, and said and gestured as if repairing something with a threaded needle.

The hello-*san* immediately returned the ripped glove to Uruo and then ruffled Uruo's long, curly hair—like most adults loved to do since he was an infant. Uruo smiled at this giant who smelled like engine oil, or a soap with unfamiliar aroma—a smell of a foreign land.

Uruo said to the hello-san, "Thank you." His face turned red, embarrassed that his English sounded funny even to himself.

Recapturing Uruo's gutsy performance, the two boys passed by the nurse's office and turned left to go to the laundry room to see Granny Shizu.

Two weeks later, on a late Saturday afternoon, the interphone in the boys' dormitory rang. Miss Hogi, the house mother, answered the call. It was Father Sainen from his office in the main building. He said that anyone who wanted to play catch wearing a real glove should come to his office. Nearly all the boys in the dormitory dashed down the zigzag stone steps to the main building. At the entrance to Father Sainen's office, they stopped abruptly.

"Come in, boys."

Marendo stepped into the office. Uruo followed. Then the rest of the boys entered.

Two medium-size cardboard boxes with foreign letters printed on them laid open in front of Father Sainen who sat in his green-cushioned office chair. The boys surrounded the boxes, transfixed by the shiny dark brown gloves that appeared much larger and sturdier than any gloves they had ever seen. At the bottom of a box were two olive gloves shaped like a cowrie shell—catcher's mitts. Uruo's gaze intensified. He leaned over and quickly counted the mitts in both boxes.

Twelve, he concluded. *Not enough for two teams.*

"Who is the best catcher among you boys?"

"Me, Father!" Uruo yelled.

Father Sainen gently threw an olive mitt to Uruo. "Now, the best pitcher?"

"I am," Marendo, keeping his head high, raised his hand. And he caught from Father Sainen a mitt that was dark brown and smaller than the olive mitt Uruo received.

"Remember, boys. These mitts belong to everyone—none of us owns them. I already spoke to Miss Hogi to keep these boxes and gloves in the storage room in your dormitory." Setting this rule, Father Sainen handed out the remaining gloves to the rest of the boys.

Uruo hopped into the olive-gray military bus parked outside the Home's white iron gate. A familiar aroma greeted him. It was the dark hello-*san*'s odor. This "American smell"—as Marendo had called it—had something open, something welcoming about it.

Marendo plunked down by Uruo.

"Where are we going?" Uruo was certain Marendo knew the answer.

"Around Mount Fuji? Father Sainen called it the 'Tent City.' I don't know what that is."

"A city built with tents?"

Marendo punched Uruo on his arm. "Smart-ass."

Uruo pushed Marendo back, which made Marendo nearly fall off the seat.

Father Sainen got on the bus and took a seat behind the blond crewcut driver in khaki uniform.

Everybody fell silent.

The engine roared.

The highway, running east and west, snaked between the Pacific Ocean on the left and mountain ranges on the right. Uruo narrowed his eyes to see if he could catch a sight of the volcanic island of Ōshima offshore. Countless whitecaps, rising and falling, accentuated the grayish-blue expanse. A long stretch of the Izu Peninsula, veiled in haze, floated on the sea, but it soon disappeared as if sunk under the waters.

Uruo watched Marendo's eyes following the mountain ranges that flew by the windows. His eyes looked crossed as he stared intensely. Uruo almost made a wisecrack about it but halted when he saw the faraway look on Marendo's face. Marendo could sometime withdraw deeply into himself—now seemed one such time.

"He doesn't know his mom and dad," Uruo murmured to Marendo's sharply chiseled profile. Marendo had never been held in mother's arms—this was unbelievable to Uruo. Although Uruo lost his mother early in his life, he had some memories of her to cherish. His dark-skinned father had vanished suddenly from his home, leaving him and his mother behind. Still, Uruo remembered this big man who loved to hold him in his hard, muscled arms, who held his tiny hand everywhere he went, and who spoke to him not knowing if his little boy understood what he was saying to him. And then there were his grandmother and his cousin who had always been part of his daily life. Uruo was born with dark skin, but he grew up nurtured in a plenty of love. And he was well aware of it; yet, sometimes, he found himself searching for it. He had to work at his adaptation into the current institutional life. A residue of resentment remained in his heart.

In contrast Marendo grew up never knowing such parental and familial closeness—his human contact had always been within the walls of St. Veronica. Marendo knew no familial love. He had no one to miss, no one to remember. Because of this, Uruo felt for him. But then Uruo envied Marendo's superior intelligence and good looks—and Uruo knew it more than anyone else. Uruo himself had no trouble in school: He hardly studied in order to get good test results.

It was well known throughout the Home that Sister Ōgin favored white, cute, and dumb children. She liked them because they would not talk back to her or ask questions—they would do whatever she told them to do.

At first Uruo suspected Marendo might be one of Sister Ōgin's favorites. But then Marendo was far from being dumb. Uruo noticed she always looked at Marendo from distance. Uruo had never seen her talking to Marendo, and Marendo had never spoken about her. He showed no fear of her, only indifference.

But Uruo feared her, ever since that first day at St. Veronica's when she threw him in the holly bush. Sister Ōgin disliked kids of color. The darker they were, the nastier she treated them. Marendo and Uruo had two close female friends at St. Veronica's: Yuri and Inga. Inga was the darkest-skinned kid in the Home and was Sister Ōgin's daily target. All of the other children knew it. Yuri was light brown and was a quick-witted buffoon. Adults got a kick out of her jokes and funny faces. If she wasn't such a skilled clown, Sister Ōgin would certainly have beaten her up, too. Uruo could not be sure that he would have the courage to rescue Yuri if that ever happened to her.

Sister Ōgin was a big, strong woman. She could send a child flying off their feet. Sometimes Uruo had the urge to slap her across her face in retaliation. Uruo was not one of Sister Ōgin's favorites. He and Marendo shared that bond.

"Why are you looking at me like that?" Marendo's voice snapped Uruo back to reality.

"Oh … just thinking," Uruo mumbled.

The bus climbed a long meandering unpaved road. Mount Fuji came into view. Uruo leaned forward and sighed at the pleated grandeur of Fuji's wide-spread skirt sloping toward the plains at its foot where khaki tents stood in orderly lines. The tents soon grew higher and larger than they first appeared when the bus rattled along into this little city of tents. The bus made a huge left turn along Fuji's skirt toward a gate guarded by three military policemen. A banner across the gate read "Camp Gotenba."

Mount Fuji had transformed from a gracefully sloped wide cone into a steep narrow slope soaring toward the summit. To Uruo, Fuji had always been synonymous with grace. But then Fuji's gracefulness was the only shape he could view from the top of the hill at St. Veronica's. Now the tall precipitous Fuji, with its aloofness and detached beauty, gave Uruo goosebumps on the back of his neck. He turned up his coat collar.

When the bus parked in front of the largest tent in the city, servicemen in their khaki uniforms with garrison hats had already been waiting in three rows. Some of them wore badges of bright colors on the right chest pockets of their jackets. Uruo guessed that their badges indicated ranks, just like on the little lead soldiers he and Marendo used to play with.

The bus's narrow double door opened inward. Father Sainen stood by the driver and called the children's names, one at a time. Each child then got off the bus. Outside, a barrel-chested officer with long brown eyelashes and red cheeks responded to Father Sainen in high pitched foreign words. Each time the officer yelled a word, a soldier in uniform came forward, took the child's hand, and together walked behind a group of waiting servicemen and stood there, smiling and trying to talk to the child.

After Marendo was called out, Uruo crossed the aisle and sat in an empty seat and watched through the window each child being matched with a soldier.

Uruo's heart drummed in his head—the thought of what to say to the hello-*san* who would pick him up tightened his neck and shoulder blades. He guessed he could say "Hello" because every hello-*san* who visited the Home had said "Hello" to the children.

"Uruo Yusa," Father Sainen called.

The red-cheeked officer responded with another new word.

Uruo was the last child to get off the bus. The dark hello-*san* from before greeted him, with his arms stretched toward him.

"Hel-lo!" This word popped out of Uruo's throat loud and clear. Then he tee-heed at his own diction.

"Hel-lo my little friend!" the soldier replied, imitating Uruo's intonation.

They hugged.

Uruo said, "Thank you twelve *mit-to*." And he squatted like a catcher in baseball would in front of the hello-*san*, gesturing as if catching a baseball with a mitt. Father Sainen had told the boys that an American serviceman donated twelve baseball gloves. Uruo knew who this serviceman was, as he had never forgotten his gentle smile and his huge hands.

"Yes, '*mit-to*.' The mits. Yes." The hello-*san* repeated Uruo's funny diction.

They hugged again. Then hello-*san* pointed to the large tent with its entrance wide open. All the serviceman/child pairs were heading toward the same entrance.

Inside the tent were four rows of long tables, each flanked by wooden chairs. Some of the plates on the tables were already filled with food. Uruo stretched but was too short to get a view of the dishes on the tables. The aroma coming out of the tent was irresistible. He anticipated he was about to taste something he had never had in his mouth.

When Uruo and the hello-*san* entered the tent full of delicious aroma, the hello-*san* pointed to a banner hanging from the ceiling above the narrow stage on the other end of the tent.

"Happy," the hello-*san* read the first word on the banner loud, turned to Uruo, and with his right hand gestured him to repeat the word. "Easter." The two words came out of Uruo's mouth, smooth and clear. The hello-*san*'s large hand squeezed Uruo's shoulder.

Suddenly a fever pricked his ears. Not because he could say these English words well. He was embarrassed at his wishful thinking that this big black man could be his father and he might take him to America when he could return home. But fever cooled just as soon as it ignited. Uruo said to himself it was nothing but a dream—the kind that evaporated with no chance of realization. A silly dead thought. The determination he had made a few years ago came back to him: No hello-*san* would request Sister Ōgin's permission to adopt him because of his uneven teeth, his body that was too husky for his age, and his skin color neither dark like Inga's nor light—it was walnut. Uruo saw himself as an unwanted animal who would be caged at St. Veronica's for six more years until he turned fifteen.

Everyone in the tent stood up, lowered their heads, and joined their hands in prayer. A man offered a monologue, which, Uruo guessed, was a prayer of some sort—but he could not tell what kind of prayer it was. Uruo turned to his black hello-*san.* His eyes were moving in every direction under his closed eyelids. And his thick lips were quivering—perhaps he was praying with the man on the stage in front of the banner that boldly displayed "Happy Easter!"

July 1962

A CAMPHOR TREE canopied the incinerator building on the east end of a hill that looked more like a cliff than a slope. Uruo had discovered this tree one day when he took two bags of garbage to the incinerator. The tree, with its rugged roots gripping into the earth, grew straight upward from the steep slope. Among its branches was a thick limb that stretched sideways, sprouting ill-shaped gnarls. These gnarls fascinated Uruo. He wanted to touch them and see how they felt against his hands, he wanted to see if there were holes inside and birds, squirrels, or even snakes were living in them. He wanted to straddle the biggest gnarl to see how the world below would look like. If the ocean lay in the south of town—as Uruo's fourth-grade teacher had said—he should see it.

To get to the gnarled limb, he needed to use other branches from surrounding trees as his footholds. These branches had grown in an upward spiral: It enabled Uruo to easily leap from one to the next. His sneakers provided good traction as he neared the gnarled limb. He had picked up these sneakers out of voluminous relief supplies that had arrived the previous Christmas from the United States. Miss Hogi had sewn onto the pair with blue woolen yarn the first letter of his last name, "Y." Other children knew Uruo owned this pair of sneakers. But the pair had already gotten tighter since Christmas.

Uruo pushed himself up onto the gnarled limb and straddled it where it forked from the trunk. There he leaned back against the trunk. The leaves were dense, and their scent pungent and chemical. Sunlight filtered through countless tiny windows the overlapping leaves created. He saw the township of Chinosaki expand southeast to meet a hazy outline of a peninsula from which extended the horizon eastward. He sighed at the quiet movement of the colossal ocean that defined the south limit of the town.

For him the ocean was an enormous blue mystery. The water knew where to go, but something had to make the water move.

Questions kept erupting in his brain. The coming and going of waves—this was unfathomable to Uruo. It seemed to him waves arrived from afar to destroy themselves, crushing into the seashore. Uruo edged forward, straddling the limb—first moving both hands, followed at the same time by both legs. By the time he arrived at the biggest gnarl at the far end of the limb, his thighs were sore: The limb was so thick that he had to open his legs wider and balance himself by tightening the grip of his thighs as he moved forward.

Uruo was disappointed that the gnarl had no holes. He knocked it lightly with his fist. The gnarl responded with a hard and dry percussive noise. There was a smooth dent in the middle of the gnarl's surface. He encircled the gnarl with his forearms, bent forward, and fit his head side way into the dent. The scent of the tree resembled mothballs, which reminded him of Nao's gray *kimono* that she had worn for the meeting with Master Kangen at the school in Mitsukaidō long ago.

Uruo moved back to the trunk. Below the gnarl limb spread a wide space with no branches. Down on the dark soil about fifteen feet below, leaves had been raked away. The custodian of the incinerator building cleaned up areas surrounding the building.

Something sparked in his brain. An idea to make a swing: one that would swing in large circular motions.

It was clear to him that the gnarled limb was going to be the central beam to which a rope would be tied. But where could he find a rope? An idea flashed in his mind: the incinerator room. Trash belonged to no one. This meant that, for whatever waste he picked up, he could claim it as his own. He was proud of this realization. Not even Marendo could have come up with this idea.

On the following Saturday, after a half-day of class, Uruo headed straight to the incinerator building. Inside it was warm. The custodian had completed the second round of garbage incineration at noon and had gone out to lunch. Uruo had learned the custodian's daily routine: He turned on the incinerator at nine in the morning, then every three hours until six in the evening. After each incineration the custodian would disappear from the building to take a break. That day, too, Uruo knew the custodian would not return to the building until twenty minutes to three. Since the entrance to the building had no door, Uruo could easily get inside.

He squatted on a thick roll of tattered mat that lay below a scorched diamond-shaped window. He scratched the burnt portion of the window with his fingernail. The texture felt rough. The charred surface did not scratch off, but instead its hard texture resisted his finger. To his far left was a well-used iron oven with its lid wide open. Curious, Uruo cautiously walked over to it. The oven mouth looked much larger than those of the steam engines that he remembered from his days in Mitsukaidō. He wanted to peek inside, but the remnant of the last incineration was still discharging its vapor out of the oven. The lukewarm reek brushed across his face. He wiped his face with his white shirt sleeve and smelled it. The rotten smell had not seeped through the shirt. If it had, Miss Hogi would interrogate him about where he had been until he confessed. He was relieved.

Covering his nose and mouth with his hand, Uruo stepped over to the other side of the oven where old doors and windows lay against the wall. These old doors looked slanted. One side of the doors rested on a rope that was neatly rolled up. He pulled out the rope from under the doors a bit at a time to let the doors fall on the concrete floor smoothly. The rope was thicker than a regular water hose, its fibers braided firm. One end of it was looped and fastened tightly with a double-layered wire. He put his arm through the roll and hooked it over his shoulder. He opened the middle window and sneaked out of the building.

The dented gnarl could be a stopper to keep the rope in the middle of the limb, Uruo estimated. The rope hung straight down. Satisfied, he climbed down the camphor tree and landed on the sloped ground at the tree's base. Stretching his upper body and arm, he grabbed the rope; and, gripping it with both hands, he kicked the tree trunk to let the rope create a counterclockwise circular motion in the air.

The rope took him far beyond the incinerator building, brushing past the brick chimney. Fifteen feet below, the dark soil outlined the foot of the slope. Every time he came around to where trunk was, he would kick it with all his power to revive the rope's circular motion and launch himself off.

The ocean seemed to have expanded farther than when he had last seen it from the camphor tree. The horizon was pushed back, which brought into his view the conical island of Ōshima—an active volcano emitting a thin strip of purple smoke. Uruo had heard that this thin smoke would gradually transform into a hazy red halo. He shuddered at the ominous image of the red halo over the island. A horror story grew in his mind: Volcano worshippers might come to the island to immolate themselves in the seething crater; and, at midnight, when the moon is full, they revive from the flame, clamber up the crater to its edge, and dance naked in a trance, twirling and twirling until the sunrise.

Uruo was dangling in midair. Above the incineration building with its concrete roof full of old dead leaves—blackish brown, flattened and wet. Captivated by his own bloodcurdling story, he had forgotten to kick the tree trunk to renew the rope's momentum. He at once measured, with his eyes, the distance between the rope and the roof and decided not to jump for the fear he might fracture his legs. Meanwhile he let the rope twirl slowly, and he did not resist it.

The gnarl creaked.

Uruo looked up.

A diagonal crack shot from the root of the gnarl into the limb's core. Uruo looked down below his feet. If the gnarl broke, he would hit the dark soil: The impact might cripple him for the rest of his life.

He quickly grabbed a massive bunch of willow branches drooping by the camphor limb, hugging it like a harvested bundle of barley.

What looked like a green log with gelid luster coiled itself among the willow branches, noiseless. Its circumference seemed about the same as Uruo's lower leg.

Uruo's arms tingled.

A green head rested on a coil, its eyes cold and its tongue flickering as if casting a spell.

Uruo's blood froze, his grip escaping. Uruo was slithering down the willow leaves.

He fell about ten feet to the rooftop of the incineration building.

"Who's there?" A girl yelled. "I know someone's up there."

The tip of a ladder appeared at the south end of the roof. A small light brown face, with semi-frizzy hair tightly bundled with a red rubber band on top of her head, peeked over the edge of the roof.

"Uruo!" The girl showed her perfectly aligned teeth. "What in the world are you doing here?"

"A snake." Fright blocked his throat. "It's huge."

"The blue-green snake?" The girl's eyes bulged. "Gosh." Both of her hands pressed over her mouth.

Uruo nodded twice, rubbing his rear, getting up to face the girl. "Come, Yuri. He's still there, I bet."

When Yuri hopped on to the rooftop from the ladder, the back of her skirt turning up, showing her thin white underwear. Her agility attested to the reputation that she was the fastest runner at St. Veronica's School. Two years older than Uruo, Yuri could beat him at least by five meters, even though he also was known to be a fast runner.

"Where?" she whispered.

Uruo gestured her to follow him. Standing under the willow branch, he searched for the snake.

"There."

A green mass of coil was moving slowly on the willow branches he had been on.

"His head isn't moving." Yuri's voice trembled. "He is looking at us. Look at that head. It looks so evil ..."

The movement of the green coil intensified.

Yuri grabbed Uruo's wrist. "Let's go to the chimney and see what it does."

"Okay."

They squatted down in front of the chimney which was still warm from the noontime incineration. Uruo thrust himself forward to watch the snake's head sway upward among the willow branches while its coiled body kept moving as if independent of the head. Then, uncoiling its body, the snake abruptly shifted the position of the head, suspending from the branch with his head slightly raised, looking at Yuri and Uruo in midair. After a moment of total stillness, the snake crashed against the rooftop.

Yuri clung to Uruo. His left arm gripped around her waist. Their feverish fear glued them together.

"Lord." Yuri quivered. "He's swallowed some eggs. Or something."

"How do you know?"

"Look at him—he's bumpy from head to tail."

Zigzagging along the east edge of the rooftop, the snake looked like it was floating through the air. It stopped, stared into the space as if in a trance, and resumed its zigzagging. Yuri and Uruo held on to each other tight and watched the snake flicker its forked black tongue.

Uruo felt Yuri's right breast pressed against his side. Holding her waist, he drew her closer to him. He spotted her parted lips.

The snake disappeared.

Yuri gently slipped out of Uruo's arm. And, stooping herself, she walked over to the edge of the rooftop, sprawled on her stomach and stretched her neck to see if the snake had dived on to the ground down below.

Yuri's light brown thighs ignited fervent twitches in Uruo's groin. He did not resist the sensation. It traveled up through his spine.

May 1963

THE IMAGE of Nao trudging along her weary way out of the Home, clawed deeply into Uruo's memory. He was saddened by the cruelty of St. Veronica's code, which discouraged family members of the children from visiting them.

Marendo, the boy who had whispered to Uruo on his first night at St. Veronica's a year and half before, had tacitly known Uruo's rage. At first he was uncertain if Uruo's anger stemmed from the school's policy of separation, or from Sister Ōgin who was the adamant enforcer of this policy. As Uruo gradually learned to trust Marendo and share what was on his mind, Marendo apprehended that Sister Ōgin herself was the root of Uruo's rage.

One day, Uruo told Marendo how Sister Ōgin had attacked him as he was running after Nao on the pebble path. He showed Marendo the lingering scars on his left temple which were now hardly visible. Marendo wanted to console him but did not know how. He had never known family: Marendo had been wrapped up in a blanket and left at St. Veronica's iron gate when he was only three days old.

"A stork dropped me here," Marendo used to say to Uruo and laugh. Uruo never knew if Marendo was kidding him.

"Did it hurt when the bird dropped you?"

"I bounced a few times."

"How did you survive?"

"I was wrapped in newspapers and a couple of blankets, I was told."

"That made you bounce?"

"Yeah." Marendo would look at Uruo, with his fisted right hand stuck in his mouth. He got joy out of teasing Uruo.

"How did they know you were there at the gate?"

"I was crying real loud. Father Sainen was in the rectory and he heard me."

"He found you and picked you up? You're lucky."

"Yeah, I guess so."

"Did he name you 'Marendo,' too?"

"I don't know. Somebody did."

"What does it mean—I mean your name. I've never heard of it."

"Father Sainen said it means 'a rare person'."

Uruo's serious face with large hazel eyes and half-opened mouth cracked Marendo up.

"Why do you laugh at me all the time?"

"You are funny—that's why."

One day Marendo said to Uruo, "You miss your Grandma and cousin, don't you?"

Uruo sat down on the *tatami* floor of the all-purpose room. He and Marendo had been looking at one of the puzzles donated by American military families. The lower corner of the puzzle was taking its shape though it gave no hint of what it would look like when completed. Uruo leaned on the wall, folding his knees against his chest and bracing them with his arms, distancing himself from Marendo.

"What's the matter?" Marendo brushed his straight light brown hair off his forehead, exposing his socketed green eyes and high bridge in between.

"Why do you ask?"

"Don't you want to see them?"

Uruo stared at Marendo as if searching for his true intention. Then he snapped, "Stop it. Don't try to be funny."

Marendo looked at the puzzle, picked up a piece that resembled a four-leaf clover, and fit it into the corresponding empty pattern on the upper-middle part of the puzzle.

"How did you know that piece would fit there?"

"I saw the pattern." Marendo raised his right knee, put his arm on it, and rested his chin on the arm, side-glancing at Uruo. "What do you think?"

"What do I think of what?"

"Your Grandma and cousin."

"I don't know." Uruo fidgeted.

"I want to meet them."

"How?"

"We'll go to where you came from." Marendo took his finger and traced it in a curved line on the floor, as if drawing a path on a map to Uruo's home.

"Mitsukaidō?"

"Of course. Isn't that where your Grandma and cousin live?"

Uruo frowned. "I don't get it."

"Come with me." Marendo stood up and headed for the lower-level floor where a large shoe cupboard for the dormitory children was located. Uruo followed Marendo.

It was a Sunday in May, late morning. The four aged cherry trees along the stone wall, now deep green without blossom, soared into the pure blue sky.

The morning Mass, presided over by Father Sainen, had completed at about eight o'clock. The children had finished their breakfast—a raw egg over a bowl of white rice and a smaller bowl of miso soup. Some boys were already out in the playground for a game of kickball.

Marendo decided not to take the gravel path because there was always someone passing by, mostly the Home's staff.

"Where are we going?" Uruo asked.`

"Follow me."

"Why don't you tell me? What's the big deal?"

The late morning sun seeped through the still foliage that canopied the descending zigzag path.

"The back door should be open," Marendo muttered as they approached the chapel.

Marendo grabbed the knob with both hands and pushed the door inward, lifting it not to let it squeak. He nodded his head to signal Uruo to go in. Uruo stepped into the concrete foyer and waited for Marendo to come in.

They looked at each other and removed their shoes at the same time. The back door of the chapel opened into a little kitchen whose waxed floor shone in subdued Philippine bronze. The smell of toast lingered in the air. Uruo imagined having a luxurious breakfast of three pieces of toast with butter, two poached eggs, and a cup of English brown tea. The sweet whiff of toast was a sign that Sister Ōgin, Father Sainen, and the Home's superintendent had had breakfast together after the morning service in the rectory connected to the chapel. This was part of their Sunday routine. Marendo put his left ear against a narrow sliding door on the left side of the foyer that separated the chapel kitchen from the rectory. No noise emanated from the rectory. Uruo followed Marendo. They sneaked out of the kitchen and made a left into the main chapel.

When the children and the staff filled the chapel, like they had early that morning, the plain wooden cross that stood between the top of the altar to the ceiling appeared not so big. But, now, standing in the empty space, the cross looked gigantic: at least four times as large as Uruo. The cross had no luster. Countless subtle grains, oblong in shape and pale brown in color, ran all over the cross, darkening the wood's cream color. The grains cast an illusion that they were quivering. This was the first time Uruo felt the chapel's stillness. He could not articulate what it was that he was sensing—reverence, peace, an embracing. If the chapel's kitchen entrance were kept unlocked and nobody was around, he could come here and just sit in a pew anytime.

"Hey, what're you looking at?" Marendo whispered to Uruo's blank face. Stepping up onto the sanctuary and turning right, Marendo opened a narrow decorative drawer attached to the bottom of the pulpit, picked up a red velvet pouch that was tied at the top, put the pouch into his back pocket, and returned to where Uruo was standing.

"What did you steal?"

"Just borrowing a key."

"To what?"

"To this." Marendo pointed at the cream door patterned with grains—like the cross on the altar. He untied the pouch and took out a silver key, weighed it on his right palm. With a heavy clank, the door unlocked. "The vestry," he told Uruo.

"The what?"

"You prepare for the service here in this room. You are allowed in if you are an altar boy. You haven't been one yet."

"Because I'm dark? Everyone else has been an altar boy."

"Stop saying that. Your turn will come." Marendo turned to a closet with a double door placed against the wall.

Uruo's heart rushed. When it stopped, he nearly fainted. A naked man, on the cross, the size of a real adult man, hung on the wall opposite the door, wearing a crown of thorns; and a streak of blood was coming out of his chest. Uruo stepped back and bumped into the entrance door of the vestry. He had seen crucifixes the size of his forearm or his palm hung on the walls of the Home's reception room and the school's hallways. But this was the first time he had ever encountered a life-size crucifix. He never knew that this terrifying statue of a condemned man had been hidden in the vestry as he had never been inside this preparation room—as Marendo put it. A halo of thorns stuck into the crucified man's forehead, his long and gaunt face bloody. Uruo covered his left temple with his hand where a holly bush scraped when Sister Ōgin had thrown him into the bush. The pain revived across Uruo's face. He rubbed the wound again.

Marendo, on all fours, stuck his neck out of the closet.

Speechless, Uruo pointed his index finger at the bleeding condemned man.

"Jesus," Marendo mumbled. "Crucifixes are everywhere in this place—you can't get away from them."

"But why some of them are just crosses, without the bleeding man?"

"I don't know. Ask Father Sainen."

Father Sainen had told the story of Golgotha with such passion, and the whole congregation listened motionless. But his story did not elicit the same kind of dramatic reaction in Uruo as seeing this grotesque mannequin: It seized him with terror.

"I want to show you something." Marendo pulled Uruo out of his fright.

Uruo stepped into the closet.

Marendo had already removed a small wooden piece at the corner of the closet floor. From underneath the floor, he took out a jar of strawberry jam packed with one-hundred-yen coins.

"Where did you find them?"

"That pottery behind you."

There was a utility shelf with boxed white and red wines, a stack of cardboard boxes, stacks of new candles for the altar—each wrapped in a sheet of cellophane paper. Near the door was a pelike pot with two handles, a narrow neck, a plain but thick mouth, and a large belly. This earthy colored pot had no picture on it, but a vague spiral pattern starting around the neck descending all the way down to the bottom.

"It's real heavy," Marendo said. He dipped his right hand into the pot and took out a handful of coins of mixed denominations. "See, Uruo, I picked only one-hundred-yen coins." He picked up the strawberry jar with his left hand: It contained only silvery coins. "I hide this jar here in the closet, under the floor."

Uruo took the jar from Marendo's left hand and try to count the coins. Marendo released the coins in his right hand back into the pelike pot.

"What do you think?"

"You're stealing the chapel's money, Marendo."

"So? What if I want to get out of here? How am I going to do that? They don't give us any money. Is this how they keep us caged in here until we are fifteen years old?"

"I never knew you felt that way." Uruo choked momentarily. He too had thought the same thing—not once, but many times.

"You have a family to go back to. I don't. I was abandoned at the gate here. I gotta do something to get out of here. No time to be a nice little obedient boy."

"But I don't think you're doing it the right way. You can't steal. If you want some money, ask Father Sainen. He will say no, though."

"Jesus, don't tell me what I can and can't do. You sound like a girl." Gripping the coin jar, Marendo glared at Uruo.

"I'm not a girl, Marendo. You know why you want to get out of here? I bet you don't even know why. You just want to get out for the sake of getting out because you don't know anywhere else except St. Veronica's. You don't care what's out there—you just want to get out of here. You know you'll be homeless."

"Shut your fat mouth, Blacky!"

Uruo swiftly laid flat on his back and kicked Marendo's chest with his right foot. The coin jar flew and landed on the wooden floor, shattering the jar and sending the coins in all directions. Marendo's back and head hit the closet wall. The wall creaked. Marendo couldn't get up. With both of his feet, Uruo locked Marendo at his shoulder bones against the wall. Then Uruo buried his foot into Marendo's stomach once.

Marendo moaned in pain and braced his abdomen.

"You think you're so smart. You are not. You're an idiot, and nobody wants you!" Uruo stood up and kicked Marendo one last time, in the knee. Then he banged the double door of the closet shut. Detouring the condemned bloody man on the cross, Uruo got out of the vestry.

September 1964

Sister Ōgin sawed Inga's cheek open.

Marendo vomited.

It happened when Marendo was, as part of his chores, sawing off an old dead limb that had grown from near the root of the barkless crape myrtle that stood thick and canopied the roof of Sister Ōgin's suite. Inga squatted near Marendo telling him how her mother danced every night at the Club Blue Moon for the Occupation officers in Yokosuka where she had been born and raised. This story was her trademark—everyone knew it. She repeated the story, but she always managed to have an audience. The audience sometimes included house mothers. Who could resist Inga's story accompanied by her fluid gestures modeled after her mother's dance? When she told her story, her voice came alive, and her eyes glared with intensity and a spark of devilishness. At the age of thirteen she knew it all. Some of St. Veronica's staff, supposedly devout Episcopalians, could not help simpering in bewilderment yet watch this little entertainer, captivated by her dark magical power.

Marendo kept on sawing the dead limb while her story continued.

Wanting more attention from Marendo, Inga stood up and demonstrated slow and sultry hip and breast motions. She had learned her dancing skills by watching her mother strip at the Club Blue Moon before the mother decided to leave Inga in St. Veronica's care.

On his knees, Marendo pulled the hand saw out of the dead limb to oil its teeth.

Inga shook her square shoulders and pear-shaped little buttocks in a rhythmical precision.

The moment Marendo chuckled, he caught sight of a blurred figure of a woman in a black suit standing inside the shadowed window, staring at Inga. He abruptly sent eye signals to Inga. She missed his signals. The figure disappeared. Marendo had no time to warn Inga.

Sister Ōgin materialized by the tree with a whoosh. Suddenly the saw was in Sister Ōgin's hand, as if it had leapt on its own from Marendo's.

Inga stepped back, her gaze glued to Sister Ōgin's eyes hidden behind her black pair of sunglasses.

Sister Ōgin stepped forward and raised the saw in a flash.

Its teeth gashed Inga's cheek wide open.

Inga's screech shook mid-September air. She fell on the ground, writhing, as blood poured out all over.

"Don't you ever think this is a cabaret your mother danced for young American soldiers. You little black bitch!"

Marendo kneeled by Inga, his undershirt removed half-way up. A sheet of blood stained her face, neck, shoulder, and chest down to the green grass. It penetrated his vision. Stunned, he dashed out to get Mrs. Mori, the nurse. Inga's screech diminished before she lost consciousness.

All the boys in the playground stopped the soccer game and froze, their faces ashen.

Uruo and Marendo had heard that Inga returned to the casualty ward of St. Veronica's from the Chinosaki Municipal hospital located about twelve miles east of the Home.

"Ten stitches, Miss Hogi said," Marendo whispered to Uruo as if disclosing a piece of classified data.

"Did it cut through her cheek?"

"Almost." Marendo looked into Uruo's eyes. "She lost a lot of blood."

"Is she all bandaged up?"

"I don't know. I haven't seen her since she came back."

"Can we visit her?"

"We can ask Mrs. Mori."

"Are you going to ask Mrs. Mori?"

"Let Yuri do it."

"Then ask Yuri to ask Mrs. Mori, Marendo."

"You ask Yuri. She likes you a lot." Marendo smirked.

"Stop it."

"So, are you going to ask Yuri or not?"

Uruo could not shut him up. "Okay, I will."

The following day, during the lunch hour at school, Yuri peeked into Uruo and Marendo's classroom. "Mrs. Mori said we could come to the nurse's office after school."

"Did you hear anything more about Inga?"

"Yes." Yuri dropped her gaze on the white tiled floor.

"What?"

"Her wound is deep. It won't go away any time soon—maybe for the rest of her life." Yuri squeezed Uruo's hand. "I'll see you later?"

Uruo nodded. He watched Yuri until she turned right at the staircase going up to the secondary school units where her classroom was.

At four o'clock, Marendo, Yuri, and Uruo gathered outside the entrance to the nurse's office. Yuri knocked on the door, loud enough to let Mrs. Mori know their arrival.

Mrs. Mori opened the door and ushered them to the round table where she had prepared a plastic cap, a mask made of thick gauze, and a pair of surgical gloves for each of them to wear. Mrs. Mori urged them to wash their hands in cresol before putting these protections on. The smell of iodine reminded Uruo of the day he had first arrived at St. Veronica's Home when Sister Ōgin threw him into the well-manicured holly bushes. The painful memory surfaced in his heart. It then melted into the agony that Inga must have gone through the moment her cheek was sawed.

Uruo put on the protective gear.

Marendo, with all the equipment already on, kept his eye on Uruo as if he was dissuading Uruo from falling into a dark memory.

Yuri was already heading for the casualty ward adjacent to the office.

"Yuri, dear. Wait for me."

"Hurry up, Mrs. Mori."

⁓

"No longer than twenty minutes, children?" Mrs. Mori said as she opened the black gauzy blinds halfway up the windows to let the early evening sun into Inga's room.

"It's me, Inga." While Yuri took Inga's frail hand in hers, Uruo shifted his glance to Inga from the pebbled path outside. "Your favorite boys are here, too."

"Who?" Inga murmured.

"Uruo and Marendo." Yuri gently let Marendo hold Inga's hand.

"Uruo?"

"I'm here, Inga."

Inga raised herself but could not sustain the posture. "Glad you boys are here." Although the right side of her face and the top of her head was covered thick with white dressing, her left eye and the left corner of her mouth signaled her silent gratitude.

"No need to hurt yourself. Don't get up." Marendo placed Inga's hand under the khaki blanket and tacked her in.

Inga cast her gentle gaze on Uruo who, in turn, patted her hand over the blanket.

Uruo withdrew his hand in awe: He had compared his own skin color with Inga's and Yuri's—walnut, black, and amber. Uruo questioned why he did this and what seized him to do such shameful comparisons. Fear or guilt?

Knowing it outrageous, he continued with his comparison. He wanted somebody to assure him his skin color was different from Yuri's and Inga's—not Marendo's because he was white: maybe even too white to be Japanese. It then occurred to him that maybe Inga, Yuri, and Uruo were too black to be Japanese. Maybe none of them belonged to the country where they all were born and raised. Sister Ōgin's favoritism allowed no sympathy for these black children: She only liked white and good-looking boys and girls. Everybody knew it. Uruo could be the next victim of a face-sawing, or she could beat him up with a baseball bat, simply because he was not white and beautiful. And even with Yuri's amber skin, she had always been grouped with other black children in Ōgin's racial calculus. Uruo resigned himself to the fact that someone's skin color were viewed as either white or black—with nothing in between. It wasn't that Yuri's comparative lightness shielded her from Sister Ōgin's wrath; it was that she could use her humor to disarm Ōgin, and if she could not, she was at least fast enough to escape her.

Uruo suddenly remembered Tomasu, his black classmate. Tomasu was almost as fast a runner as Yuri, and almost twice big as Uruo—and Uruo was pretty big for a boy. One Sunday in late October last year, something bad happened to Tomasu. The children were required to attend a Mass that morning. Tomasu got up late so he had no time to brush his teeth, wash his face, and empty himself. During the services, he kept passing gas—some were soundless with a dreadful odor; others sounded like air going out of tire. Nothing could stop the children from laughing. After the services, Sister Ōgin got out of the chapel as fast as she could and waited in the chapel's front yard, holding a short-handled broom. When Tomasu came out of the chapel, Sister Ōgin beat him with the broom. Tomasu's face turned dark purple with rage. He seized the broom handle, snatched it out of her hand, and smacked her with it on the buttocks with all his might at least four times. Tomasu then threw the broom at her and ran on the pebbled path straight back to his dormitory. Sister Ōgin chased after Tomasu wearing a pair of shiny black high heels. The heels got buried in the pebbles. She fell, her legs pointing the sky. The children laughed and laughed. No one saw Sister Ōgin and Tomasu for the next few days. Then there was a rumor that Tomasu had been sent to a juvenile reformatory—a punishment in exile. Tomasu never came back to St. Veronica's.

"What—tell me, Uruo," Yuri whispered.

"I just remembered something."

"What?" Marendo asked.

"C'mon, tell us." Inga's hoarse voice urged Uruo.

"Remember, Tomasu?" Uruo said. "I miss him."

"Me, too," Yuri and Marendo said in unintended duet.

Silence fell.

"You think Sister Ōgin will ship me to a reform school?" Inga sounded feeble and fearful.

"I doubt it," Marendo chimed in. "If she sends you away, people will see your cheek and ask why the wound and ask what's going on at St. Veronica's. She can't say tree branches scratched your cheek. She must let you stay here until you are fifteen."

"He's right," Yuri said. "She's got a few kids to hide, for sure."

"Including me."

"You?" Yuri was taken aback.

"Yeah. See this?" Uruo pointed his left temple where the wound was, now hardly visible.

"Gosh, I never knew." Yuri traced Uruo's wound with her fingers.

Uruo let her touch his face, his gaze focused on Inga.

"I hope Sister Ōgin has not added reformatory to her list of punishments," Yuri said.

"You never know. No one has been shipped to a reformatory after Tomasu, though." Marendo affirmed.

"I hope she's forgotten about reformatory," Yuri said, holding Inga's hand. Inga moaned slightly.

"She's on painkillers. Maybe we should let her alone," Mrs. Mori said.

They removed their caps, masks, and surgical gloves and put them back on the round table.

"Inga is going to sleep," Yuri reported to Mrs. Mori.

"Let her." Mrs. Mori stepped over to the entrance to open the door.

"We'll be back," Marendo said.

"You let me know when."

Yuri went out first. Marendo followed. Uruo closed the door behind him.

Yuri backed, and bumped into Marendo. She was stock-still. Sister Ōgin was coming out of the main office. All three of them stood motionless, anticipating she would come toward them. Uruo was certain Yuri would take care of the situation if that would happen. Sister Ōgin headed in the opposite direction toward the main kitchen. They sighed in relief, knowing she was returning to her suite through the back way.

"Where is Father Sainen?" Marendo broke the silence, looking at the corner of the office building where Sister Ōgin had turned.

"Why?" Yuri was quick.

Both Marendo and Yuri turned to Uruo.

"Isn't he supposed to be doing something? Like talking to Sister Ōgin about what happened to Inga?" Uruo asked.

"I don't know." Marendo answered. He continued, but in a low pitch: "You know, it seems every time Sister Ōgin punishes a kid, Father Sainen is not around."

"That's not true, Marendo," Uruo said. "When Sister Ōgin hurt me, he came out of the reception room to help me." Uruo rubbed his wound on the temple. "Didn't he find you at the gate twelve years ago?"

"Yeah, I know all that. But … I … don't know, there's something weird about the whole thing."

"Like what?" Yuri stepped in. "Like he is a friend of Sister Ōgin's? I mean, like they sleep together?"

"I don't believe it." Uruo grimaced.

"What do you mean 'I don't believe it'? He is a man, isn't he?" Marendo said. "You should know that much, at least." Marendo was put off by Uruo's innocence—perhaps feigned innocence, he suspected.

"Maybe he and Sister Ōgin work together well," Yuri said. "Mrs. Mori once told me they both went to college in London."

"No matter what, Ōgin is the master here." Marendo sounded like a young elderly—wise and worldly.

Marendo's words reminded Uruo of the gigantic snake that he and Yuri had encountered on the rooftop of the incinerator building. The snake that embodied an evil spirit with its cold blood and trance-like indifference. But it seemed to Uruo that there was only one master snake at St. Veronica's, and its name was Ōgin.

June 17, 1965

TWO YEARS before, when Uruo was eleven, Marendo had shocked him with a jarful of one-hundred-yen coins which Marendo had transferred bit by bit from the pelike pot kept in the chapel's vestry. Whether Marendo had kept amassing his savings after their confrontation that day, Uruo was uncertain. Marendo had never said anything about it since. Neither had Uruo. Uruo did not want Marendo's savings to cause another fight between them—once was enough. Uruo surmised nonchalance was Marendo's tactic. But Uruo's curiosity grew until he could no longer contain it.

"How much do you have now?" Uruo did not stop pushing his bamboo broom as he swept the zigzag stone slope on the south side of the hilltop that connected down to the main office.

"What do you mean?" Marendo kept on sweeping slightly behind Uruo.

"You know—your savings."

"My savings?" Marendo smirked. "I like that: 'savings.' Make it 'our' savings." This time he did not look at Uruo. "What's the matter?"

"Nothing."

"You're lying, Uruo." Marendo stopped sweeping. His penetrating green eyes probed into Uruo's motive for asking about his savings for the first time in two years. "It's the time to use some of it, isn't it?"

"Stop, Marendo. Let me do my chore alone."

Marendo ascended the zigzag slope to the boys' dormitory.

After he had finished sweeping, Uruo ran to the camphor tree, climbed it, and straddled over the limb with the half-cracked gnarl. He leaned back against the tree trunk. This spot on the tree had become his sanctuary where he could be away from his thirteen "brothers" in the boys' dormitory and from the Home's staff members whom he had to greet when he passed. He disliked adult folks because their attitudes changed like kaleidoscopes. They pitched their voices differently according to whom they were speaking, they altered their facial expressions according to whom they were looking at, and this always changed depending upon where in the staff hierarchy of the Home they stood. In this staff hierarchy, as Uruo had learned it, there was a system of reporting among the staff. When a report about a student's bad behavior reached Father Sainen, he gently reprimanded the child in question; and the matter progressed no further. But some of the other staff members' reports went up the hierarchy and reached Sister Ōgin who, in turn, punished the problem child. And the darker the children, the harder the punishment: This was the Home's unwritten axiom. So Uruo stayed away from adults as much as he was able.

Through the cream-green leaf buds around him, Uruo could see the ocean, turquoise and motionless. A dot emerged on the horizon, and it grew into a shape of a bow. The ship grew larger: It was coming toward the shore. But it made a wide U-turn back to the horizon. And it disappeared beyond the fine gray line that divided the sky and the sea. Uruo's gaze remained at where the ship had gone out of sight. Every time he straddled over this branch and watched the ocean, the horizon convinced him there was *something* beyond, though he could not imagine what that something could be.

Marendo never talked about anything invisible. Maybe it was too much of a fairy tale for him. If Marendo wanted to, he could have created some captivating stories. Marendo could write. Their creative writing teacher always used his writing as an example. She never used Uruo's, though he had secretly hoped that someday she would use his as a model. Her standoffish gaze bothered him. A cool distance stood between them. His walnut skin, Uruo surmised, might have created this distance.

Leaves made a rough rustle above Uruo's head. Once … twice … as if to draw his attention. Uruo looked up. No one was there. But the leaves soughed harder.

Someone perched on the limb where Uruo straddled, and nimbly faced Uruo. It was Marendo: "Thought you'd be here looking at the ocean."

"You're bothering me."

"I don't think I am."

"What you want?"

"Not what I want. But what you want. And you know it."

"You're right. You're always right. Sometimes it gets to me."

"I don't know how much I have, but I have four jars of coins now. I can probably take thirty one-hundred-yen coins out of our savings, easily. Do you think that's enough?"

"No idea, Marendo."

"Let's go to the train station—it's right across the Home's gate. We'll look at the maps and the fare list. Oh, the schedule, too."

"Now?"

"If not now, when?"

"Do we have to go to the chapel first?" Uruo shuddered to think he'd have to revisit that place with its hideous effigy of Christ, where he and Marendo had come to blows and shattered that jar of coins all over the floor.

"No need." Marendo clinked his pockets.

Uruo climbed down the trunk. Marendo followed.

A county bus parked in a lot between the train station and the public lavatory, waiting for its departure time to head for Hirano. The moment Uruo and Marendo stepped out of the Home's gate, Marendo came up with the idea of first taking the bus to the nearest town from Chinosaki, which was Hirano. And Uruo at once agreed to this idea which, he thought, was brilliant.

Six employees, including the stationmaster, managed the Chinosaki train station. Every employee knew the faces of most of the St. Veronica children, which meant they were familiar with both Uruo and Marendo. Their familiarity with the children stemmed from their participation in setting up logistics for field trips with the Home through the Prefectural Welfare Department.

The Home's board members, together with St. Veronica's Elementary and Junior High teachers, encouraged the children to go outside the Home for field trips. The board had proclaimed that field trips provided the children with various opportunities to see and learn what was happening outside the stone walls that surrounded the Home's estate. This proclamation was issued after due consideration that some of the children might face bullying because of their distinct non-Japanese features; however, field trips must be a necessary part of their overall learning process as they must set out on a journey into adult world when they turned fifteen. Both Uruo and Marendo had two more years left until this journey. If the employees at the train station saw the boys taking a trip alone, they'd surely detain them and call Father Sainen. Or worse, Sister Ōgin. But the bus drivers would have no particular reason to question them: A paying customer was a paying customer.

It was about twelve-thirty in the afternoon when the two boys got on the bus. Marendo paid the bus fare for the two, thirty-five yen each. The driver looked at them. They had never seen this driver. This unfamiliarity relieved Uruo.

"Let's sit in the back," Uruo said.

"Because you are dark?" Marendo stopped. "No, we'll sit right behind the driver." He took two long strides to the seat he had already selected in his head and bounced onto it. "Sit," Marendo said, patting the empty seat space by him.

Uruo cast a side glance at seven women seated in the middle of the vehicle. One with a long summer one-piece with a narrow-brimmed straw hat was looking at the platform in the train station. The rest of them focused their scornful silence on Uruo. He glared back at them until they averted their stare.

After ten minutes riding along the coast of the Pacific Ocean, Uruo and Marendo arrived at the bus terminal of Hirano Station. Marendo hurried off the bus and ran into the train station, the coins in his pants pocket jingling. Not even five minutes after going over the timetable, the map, and the fare list, he was at a ticket window where an elderly clerk waited on customers. She spoke to Marendo. He responded quickly. As she handed him two tickets, she praised the fluency of his Japanese expression, thinking he was a foreign visitor. Thanking her for the tickets, he waved at her, a gentle gesture of good-bye. She bowed. The next moment he was already grabbing Uruo by his arm and was heading to the ticket examiner at the entrance to the eastbound platform.

"Where's my ticket?" Uruo asked.

"I got it." Marendo poked Uruo's back. "C'mon."

"Man …"

"What?"

"Why the hurry?"

"You want to see your grandma and cousin, don't you?"

"Yeah, but why push me around?" Uruo complained. At the same time he admired Marendo's quick thinking, his well-defined masculine face, and his white skin that would instantly attract grown-ups. Yet, despite it all, Marendo kept his distance from everyone—his classmates and the staff, except Uruo and Father Sainen. This puzzled Uruo.

An orange dot appeared. The dot grew larger, its front windows reflecting the sun. The square face of the electric train resembled a grasshopper with a hard, angular look. The train's glass face was now enormous. And it slid into the platform.

Twelve cars filled the entire length of the platform. Their doors opened. Uruo looked at Marendo, who had hopped into the third car. Uruo's toe hit the threshold of the same entrance, and he stumbled into the car, nearly falling to the floor.

"Want the window side?"

"You take it, Uruo."

"Okay."

In a minute the doors closed, and the train glided forward. The landscape began to fly off out of Uruo's vision.

⁓

The Mitsukaidō station building had been renovated with concrete. And its floor had been tiled with cut stones. The wooden wall on the west side had been replaced with a picture window. Inside, the sun provided plenty of light. The entrance to the station had been widened. From there Namiki Street stretched straight northward.

"Shouldn't we go back?" Uruo asked, feeling suddenly out of place in his hometown.

"Do you remember how to get to your house from here?"

"Yeah, but …"

"Let's go then." Marendo got out of the station first. "Is this the street? There's only one here, anyway."

Uruo nodded, amazed at Marendo's guts to set foot in a town he had never known.

Uruo at once saw his hometown so different from five years ago. He wondered if the funny-looking stone across Chisa's house was still there. And his grandmother, Cousin Hanbo, and even angry Aunt Kureo. Uruo was certain Aunt Kureo still despised him for having been born. Yet, Uruo wanted to see them all. But somewhere in his heart was a voice telling him that he should not see them at all.

"I want to go back to Chinosaki."

"No, you don't."

"What if they aren't there anymore?'

"Let's go to your house and see if they are there first. Then you can cry if they are gone. And then we'll go back to Chinosaki."

"I hope they aren't there."

"Gee, what a girl."

"Zip it up, moron."

"We're going to your house, and that's that."

Uruo said nothing. He widened his strides and quickened his pace, letting Marendo follow behind him. At the trapezoidal stone, he stopped and looked across Namiki Street. A dozen or so bamboo brooms stood outside the sliding glass doors. And incandescent lights illuminated inside this general store. This was still a familiar sight for Uruo.

The unchanged storefront eased his tension.

"What are you looking at? Where is your house?"

"A block away." Uruo brushed sand dust off the trapezoidal stone to see if its color had maintained the same luster. It had. He resumed walking ahead to the house.

"When we come back, let's stop by that bakery by the station. It smelled so good."

"That's Uncle Gen's. I'd like that."

"Oh, I remember you telling me going there with your grandma."

"He used to give us bread crusts."

"He sounds like good man."

Uruo stopped, ignoring Marendo. He stared at a weather-beaten wooden tag nailed to the pillar on the right side of the closed entrance. The tag read: The House of Yusa. Uruo sensed Marendo's gaze at his temple.

"Open the door," Marendo commanded in whisper.

"The bell will ring real loud."

"You want me to do it?"

Uruo touched the door with no knob. He slid it open leftward. The bell chimed once and echoed. He expected noise from inside the house, but only silence echoed. He slid the door further to the left and rang the bell again. The inner entrance to the house opened and a young woman crossed the doorsill.

She abruptly covered her mouth with her hands, staring at the two foreign faces—one dark, the other light—standing on the other side of the sliding entrance. "Heavens! It's my little Uruo, isn't it?" she yelled.

"Chisa!"

They hugged. Neither wanted to let the other go.

"Grandma's here. Hanbo will be back in a while. He went to the pharmacy to get medicine for Grandma."

"Isn't she sick?"

"She got a virus last week. Still coughing. Otherwise, she's fine."

They let go of each other.

"Chisa, this is my buddy, Marendo."

Marendo bowed to Chisa, formal and charming at once. Marendo's unexpected demeanor stunned Uruo since properness had never been part of Marendo's behavior. Chisa's eyes shrunk into a pair of short threads. "Grandma is sunbathing on the veranda. She loves it out there. Let's go through the backyard." She put her right arm around Uruo's shoulders and her left arm around Marendo's.

They turned left on to the narrow dirt path space between the wooden fence and the house, stepping from stone to stone toward the bath hut and the nearby well. Uruo freed himself from Chisa and touched the well's handle, then pulled it up and down. Water gushed out of it with a familiar noise. He remembered how he wanted to play with this handle when he was five years old but could not—he was too small. He turned to the southwest corner in the yard: The persimmon tree stood there taller and thicker. The neighbor's tortoiseshell cat ran across the yard, got under the wooden fence, and disappeared. The hencoop was no longer there, but its roof line remained visible along the wall of Aunt Kureo's room. Uruo listened for her knitting machine.

On the veranda was a little woman with stooped shoulders and shiny silver hair rolled up neatly on top of her head, sitting on a floor cushion with a green-and-yellow splashed pattern, dozing. Chisa pushed Uruo forward, gently toward the veranda. Marendo stayed behind Chisa.

Uruo stood at the edge of the veranda, in front of the dozing woman.

"Grandma …," Uruo said to himself. Then the same silent word became a real voice.

She did not hear him.

Uruo sat by her and touched her folded knee and called her again, this time slightly louder than before, and patted the back of her hand. She opened her eyes and raised her head and looked at Chisa standing by the well. At that moment, she saw the dark husky thirteen-year-old boy, with a pair of large, almond-shaped eyes, sitting by her, smiling.

"Oooooh…" Her voice trembled and her eyes welled at once. "My baby, Uruo."

"Grandma." Uruo threw himself in her open arms, her faint heartbeat echoing against his face. "My Grandma," Uruo said again as if to remind himself of who she was. Suddenly, he was sobbing. His entire body relaxed in her bosom. And her natural smell confirmed that it was truly his grandmother who was embracing him now. Her smell had exorcised all fears from within and all aggressions from without. It was the smell of reassurance that had protected him every night at bedtime when he laid between her and Cousin Hanbo.

"Where's Cousin Hanbo, Grandma?"

"He'll be back soon."

"And Aunt Kureo?"

Nao hesitated. "She's no longer with us." She sighed. "I never thought you'd remember her after all this time, son."

"Of course. She was Hanbo's mom."

"Yes, she was. She never got over your uncle's passing." Nao paused, then continued in a resigned tone. "Toward the end, she hardly ate. She worked, and worked, to death. The knitting machine was the only thing she left behind."

Uruo remained in an embrace with Nao. Over her thin shoulder, he peeked at Marendo. Chisa held him close by.

"Look, son. Chisa is Hanbo's wife now."

Just then the outer entrance door slid open with force and the ringer shrilled, shattering the stillness in the house. Uruo and Nao turned to the entrance, still holding on to each other.

"This is the Mitsukaidō police, Mrs. Yusa," a voice called. "Is your grandson here?"

Nao recognized the voice as a local policeman from Mitsukaidō.

A second voice spoke up. "I am from the Mitsukaidō Juvenile Welfare Department," it said, "Father Sainen requested we retrieve your grandson and his friend. They must return to Chinosaki at once."

June 18, 1965

NOBODY, NOT even the staff members, knew that Uruo and Marendo had returned to the Home until early the next morning when the other children saw the two boys blindfolded and tied to the crape myrtle tree in front of Sister Ōgin's executive suite. Uruo and Marendo looked as if they were hugging the tree together from opposite sides. Uruo's arms stretched straight and his hands held Marendo's upper arms; Marendo's arms extended the same way Uruo's did and his hands gripped Uruo's upper arms. They were roped to the tree at their hips and ankles. The five windows of the girls' dormitory had never had this many young bewildered faces staring through them. Even the boys had run down from the hilltop dormitory into the girls' dormitory as the word had spread that Uruo and Marendo had come home after their sudden disappearance the day before.

When the morning sun began illuminating the grove of pine trees beyond the playground, Sister Ōgin appeared from her suite, with a cat-o'-nine-tails. She wore a pair of sunglasses, a black pantsuit with a black turtleneck and a black pair of high heels, with their heels extra high. With a whip dangling on her side, she prowled around the tied boys: first half circle, then the whole circle.

She stopped behind Uruo.

His shoulder muscle tightened.

The whip landed across his back, making a dull, echoless thud.

Uruo's back twitched in a spasm.

At the windows the girls clung to each other, breathless.

Sister Ōgin opened her legs further apart, rested the whip on her left shoulder, and thrust it down diagonally on to Uruo's mid-body twice in succession.

A violent tremor ran across his body, momentarily subsided, but then returned with a vengeance. Nine rouge welts, as if clawed by an iron rake, swelled up across his back. For a moment Sister Ōgin gazed at the whip. She then circled the tree counterclockwise, returned to Uruo's side, and gave a sudden blow that was heavier than before. Six more lashings followed.

Some of the welts broke open and blood oozed out.

She stood still behind Uruo as if worshiping the blood seeping out of this walnut-colored young male body. Uninhibited by her surroundings, her left hand stroked her inner thigh.

She half-circled to Marendo's side. She dropped a precisely aimed blow on Marendo's mid-back.

Marendo screamed, his head thrashing back.

Four more consecutive blows followed.

Marendo's fingers dug into Uruo's upper arms. His cry turned into wheezing. Then from his wheezy scream rose a prayer: "Our Father, who art in heaven. Hallowed be thy name. Thy kingdom come—"

Marendo's prayer only enraged Sister Ōgin. Her nine-tailed whip danced in the air, drawing the letter X with violent force.

Marendo fell silent.

At that moment, from the girls' dormitory, a black girl charged straight at Sister Ōgin. "Leave them alone!"

Sister Ōgin dodged.

The girl tumbled against the ground, dust in her mouth.

"Inga, no!" A girl inside the window yelled.

A torrent of whipping was already falling on Inga. She fought to snatch at the whip from Sister Ōgin.

Meanwhile, Mrs. Mori flew out of the girls' dormitory and untied Uruo and Marendo. Following Mrs. Mori's urgent order, Uruo positioned himself behind Marendo to catch his flaccid body—the bloody welts on his back shooting pain up into the base of his skull.

With Uruo holding Marendo's ankles, and with Mrs. Mori supporting his shoulders, they laid Marendo on the grass area between the crape myrtle tree and the entrance to the girls' dormitory. Mrs. Mori stood up, grabbed a syringe hidden in her apron, and removed the cap off the needle.

Inga bit Sister Ōgin's right wrist and did not let it go until the whip dropped on the ground. Inga picked it up quickly and threw it. The whip hit the decorative stone across Sister Ōgin's suite and bounced on the ground. Mrs. Mori, with her left arm, locked Sister Ōgin by her upper abdomen; and, with her right hand, she stabbed the needle into Sister Ōgin's right buttock. As soon as she pulled the needle out of Sister Ōgin, Mrs. Mori, with her right thumb and index finger, removed the needle from the syringe. The needle dropped on the grass. She threw the syringe back in her apron pocket.

Screaming, Sister Ōgin turned around and gave Mrs. Mori a furious high-heel kick on her thigh. Ignoring the impact of the kick, Mrs. Mori turned Sister Ōgin around and locked her by the chest. By the time they were at the entrance to Sister Ōgin's suite, Sister Ōgin's eyes rolled back and she collapsed in Mrs. Mori's arms. Leaving Sister Ōgin inside her suite by the entrance, Mrs. Mori ran back to where Uruo was whispering to Marendo on his hands and knees, fearing that Marendo would not wake up.

At the southwest corner of the main building, Yuri popped out holding a folded stretcher. "Inga, help me!" Her shriek shook the air.

Inga ran to Marendo. Yuri opened the stretcher; and together they turned Marendo over on his stomach so that his welts would not touch the stretcher. They slid him onto the stretcher. The two girls lifted the stretcher. Two boys jumped out of the windows; and, barefooted, they grabbed the middle of the stretcher, one on each side. They headed for the nurse's office.

Uruo, shivering and limping, holding on to Mrs. Mori's arm, followed them. The pain on his back kept him bent. His welts had opened and threads of blood trickled down through his underwear, soaking it red.

"Chilly in here," Marendo groaned.

"Thank God!" Mrs. Mori stopped applying the lukewarm compress to Uruo's back and turned to Marendo.

Uruo raised his head to make sure it was Marendo who complained. He had to know for sure the voice was real, not a hallucination. "You've come back, man."

"Your left side is done, Uruo," Mrs. Mori said. "I'm going to take care of Marendo's right side now. Then I'll get back to you for your right. For the next few days, I'll do it by turns—the best way."

"You're the boss, Mrs. Mori," Uruo mumbled and looked at Marendo who was studying Uruo's face. Uruo saw a ray of relief in Marendo's tortured green eyes, silently signaling, "I'm glad you are here with me, Uruo."

Uruo gave him a slight nod. "Go back to sleep."

From time to time, Marendo's back twitched and his face furrowed in pain.

Uruo surmised that Marendo had received a more severe beating than he did, and far worse when his prayer fueled Sister Ōgin's anger. Uruo was certain that Marendo had died: Marendo did not hear Uruo's voice, he did not sense Uruo's hand touching his. He just lay there on the grass like a straw scarecrow. Uruo wasn't sure if he was breathing. He prayed to God to not let him die. He wanted God to hear him. He prayed hard—his first serious prayer in his whole life. Uruo promised God that if he could let Marendo come back to life he would never sleep during the Mass services on Sundays.

Uruo, despite their past fights, wanted Marendo to be his friend even when they grew up, got married, and had their own children. Marendo was his brother. Uruo wanted to hug him right then and there. Marendo had stolen and saved money because he knew Uruo wanted to go home to his grandmother and Hanbo. That was why he endured that punishment. Marendo knew he would be whipped if he took Uruo to Mitsukaidō. Uruo regretted not having said no to him. Uruo blamed himself for Marendo suffering. His pain was so deep that prayer came out of his mouth. Uruo wondered if Marendo heard his own prayer—maybe he had already fainted.

A thought flashed across Uruo's mind: Had Marendo died and seen God? Uruo had to ask Marendo about it someday. Father Sainen always said that God was not like a man with a long white beard, but was everywhere, in everything: He *was* everything. Uruo had been skeptical of such a vague notion. He'd seen pictures of the Buddha at Zenchō-ji Temple, and the grisly image of Christ dead on the crucifix. Surely God was a person just like him. Maybe he even had dark skin.

Uruo was puzzled by why Marendo's prayer had made Sister Ōgin so enraged. It was like she lost her mind, beating Marendo like he was a tree. Didn't Sister Ōgin want to hear his prayer? She was supposed to be a woman of the Lord. She looked so pious in her black veil, joining her hands in prayer every Sunday in Mass. She would be the first to walk over to the altar and go down on her knees to receive communion from Father Sainen. Then she would bow so deep that her whole body shrank to the size of a tumbleweed. She was always first. Would it be because she was the head of the Home? Would it be because she was from a rich aristocratic family that everyone was afraid of her? It would be like an actress doing a solo performance on stage. When she would do this, Uruo could not help noticing her fingers. The red manicured nails—they scared him. He remembered she used to pinch his cheek with those sharp red nails when he was in first grade. Some of her nails dug into his skin. It hurt.

"Okay, now, your right side, Uruo." With a thick warm piece of gauze the size of a hand, Mrs. Mori touched Uruo's back. She pressed the gauze gently against the wounds and held it several seconds before moving on to the next position. Mrs. Mori's gauze brought back to Uruo the immediate memory of the whip's whistle and the pangs that pierced his skin.

Two months after the whipping, Uruo's welts healed, but the scars from the whip's fine claws remained. Marendo's wounds took longer than Uruo's to get better. The welt on the upper left shoulder got infected. Mrs. Mori had to take him to a dermatologist in town to have the pus drained. The doctor ordered Marendo to refrain from hard activity like running, heavy lifting for two more weeks.

Father Sainen returned from a two-week lecture tour—his annual event for fund raising. During his tour, he gave lectures at Episcopalian churches and colleges in all the prefectures from Hokkaido down to Kumamoto. His earnings provided enough to get Christmas gifts for all of St. Veronica's children. In addition, each child older than five years of age received a large fried chicken leg for dinner, with a side of mixed vegetables and a bowl of brown rice.

On the first Sunday after his return, Father Sainen held the Eucharist. The chapel entrance remained wide open after this day.

One Sunday, after the service, Father Sainen called Uruo and Marendo. The three of them sat in the front pew, Father Sainen between the two boys.

"Father, I'm so sorry." Marendo looked ashen, his voice trembling.

"Me, too." Uruo glanced at Father Sainen's side view.

"You need not say anything, boys. I called you up here to ask you something, and you tell me if you like what I have to say. My proposal, Uruo, is that you work at the main kitchen Monday through Friday, two hours each day. You like food, I know. And you will earn five hundred yen a month. Now, Marendo: You excel in math. How would you like to tutor two pupils in your class who are struggling with algebra? You help them Monday through Friday, one hour per pupil. The school will pay you five hundred yen each month. If you'd like to save your earnings, I can help you start a simple savings account at the post office. What do you say?"

"I'd like that idea, Father. I'd like to save my money." A rouge complexion came back to Marendo's face.

"Me, too."

"Good. You will be paid on the last day of each month, just like our staff members. We will go to the post office when you get paid this month. All settled?"

"Thank you, Father," the two boys said at the same time.

Outside the chapel, they headed for the north side of the zigzag slope, walking mechanically as if controlled by remote control like one of the little toy cars Sainen had bought for the Home. They were silent. Uruo wanted to know what was on Marendo's mind. Marendo seemed as if in a trance. At the second bend of the slope, Uruo stopped. He hated it when Marendo withdrew into himself like that. Uruo resented being ignored. But then he knew it was not Marendo's fault: it was part of how he was—ever since he'd known him.

Marendo at last realized Uruo was standing far down the slope. "C'mon, let's get back to the dorm."

"What's the money for?" Uruo shot it out, indifferent.

"What?" Marendo stopped, shocked by Uruo's locution. Marendo had never known Uruo could seem so cold. "What are you talking about?" Marendo descended the slope halfway toward Uruo.

"You know damn well what I'm talking about."

"Yeah, I do. Sorry." Marendo faced Uruo. "You are wondering what Father Sainen's offer meant, right?"

Uruo did not respond.

"I was thinking the same thing, Uruo. I mean, if there is some intention behind Father Sainen's offer—you know?" Marendo kept rubbing the sole of his right shoe against the stone step as if cleaning off manure. "Or, maybe it's just his way of educating us kids not to steal money from the chapel. Setting up for us how to earn money the right way and appreciate it."

"We both had the crap beaten out of us, Marendo. We have the proof—the scars on our back. We almost lost you." Uruo turned to the chapel. "Father Sainen wasn't there that day. I didn't see him. Then he disappeared for two weeks: Fund raising—they said. He came back. And, in front of the altar, he made the offer—we work and earn money for our services."

"We may be reading into something we don't have the slightest idea about, Uruo."

"After all that, how can you not doubt his offer?"

"I've never heard you talk like this."

"I'm angry. My gut tells me there is something behind all this. This all sounds too good to be true. Other kids don't get this kind of offer from Father Sainen. Why only us? Why aren't we in reform school, like Tomasu?"

"You mean, like, the work cages us in here? And the money encourages us to keep silent about the whipping?"

"So you knew it this whole time, Marendo!" Tears of vexation, tepid like blood, welled up in Uruo's eyes.

August 1965

Every week, Monday through Friday, Uruo got up at four-thirty to help in the main kitchen. He thought it a waste of time to wash his face. When eye mucus bothered him, he rubbed it off with his middle finger. The mucus had always hardened by the time he woke up; it made its removal easy. He never missed brushing his teeth—he could not stand his own bad breath, a smell of spoiled miso soup. He spent five solid minutes brushing his teeth in the way Mrs. Mori had taught him: first, upper teeth—front from left to right then back in the same direction; then, lower teeth—both front and back in the same directions. He liked this methodical routine and the glassy sensation in his mouth after he had cleaned his teeth. He then dashed out of the boys' dormitory and ran down the zigzag path into the kitchen.

The sky was still dark purple. The naked bulbs on the lamp-posts around the kitchen building were still glimmering like dying candles. Mr. Daigo, the chief chef, was already in the kitchen, washing rice that had been soaked in water overnight in three large cauldrons for the Home's entire population. Uruo minced onions, carrots, dried sardines, and kelp for miso soup while Mr. Daigo took care of the rice. Uruo had not acquired the knack for the right temperature and the length of cooking time so that the rice would come out both fluffy and sticky enough.

From time to time, Mr. Daigo would call Uruo to the concrete furnace with three large holes on top of it where the three cauldrons would fit in. And he would say, "Feel the heat. Shouldn't be too hot. Let it cook slow and easy." For about a month, the flame temperature appeared inconsistent to Uruo. There didn't seem a set temperature he should use as a gauge for cooking rice. When Uruo challenged Mr. Daigo as to why he used no thermometer, Mr. Daigo said that nothing could be more accurate than human senses, and that this skill would develop in time—his body would eventually receive a signal from the flame.

Once two children from each dormitory and a couple of staff members arrived at the pick-up window in the kitchen and received their rice, miso soup, and pickled vegetables in large tin containers for their respective groups, Uruo's morning duty ended. Mr. Daigo's two assistants took over the work for the remainder of the day.

But Uruo had one more hour of kitchen duty between seven and eight in the evening. There was nothing creative about his evening duty: washing all the empty tin containers returned to the pick-up window and the three steel cauldrons that had cooked rice for the entire population in the Home. The kitchen was equipped with a spacious washroom with a slanted concrete floor for two drains at the lower end. This room was attached to the back of the main kitchen, its two tall windows providing visual access to the zigzag path going up and down to and from the boys' dormitory on the hilltop and the east corner of its roof line. Uruo used a powdered, odorless, gray detergent and a pot scourer made of soft metal. Inside the entrance to this room was an old table that stored up a dozen or so boxes of pot scourers, for each wash quickly decomposed the scourer's sharpness for scrubbing and the next wash demanded a new scourer. Uruo worked barefooted, relishing the rubbing sensation of the hot water shooting out of the hose he held.

Once Marendo pointed out to Uruo that his feet had no smell like other boys in the dormitory and he wanted to know why. Uruo laughed at him and said, "I wash them every day for one hour." From that day on, Marendo would stop by the washroom from time to time and help Uruo, and he would also delight in the gentle flow of the hot water massaging his odd-shaped bare feet. Uruo nicknamed them the "eggplant feet." Marendo grimaced every time Uruo called him by this nickname. Soon this nickname spread among his classmates and older children.

Uruo surmised that, despite his grimace, Marendo enjoyed it when they teased him—especially when Yuri called him "Eggplant." Yuri's teasing made Marendo blush, but Marendo's green eyes quietly invited Yuri to come closer to him and tease him more. Marendo seemed to want Yuri's touch, like she had always touched Uruo when she talked to him as if he were her little brother. Uruo wished he had Marendo's unaffected magnetism to captivate Yuri—the magnetism that radiated from Marendo's well-chiseled white face which had been maturing into manhood in recent years. But Uruo, ever since he was an infant, had always found himself in the center of attention wherever he was. Despite his stocky build, his face never lost its child-like innocence. Uruo was "cute"—that's what older girls always said. And this cute short boy with a walnut skin was always accessible for everyone to touch. But Uruo disliked it when other children treated him like a pet.

Marendo was a natural magnet, and Uruo a natural mascot. Marendo had no interest in being anyone's mascot: He wanted girls to sense the signals of natural male sensuality he sent out. Marendo imagined that Yuri received his signals. But she did not reciprocate his signals, which put Uruo at ease. Both boys pretended that Yuri was no more than their friend. Neither one wanted to think of the day Yuri must graduate from St. Veronica's school, which was set for early next April.

That year the summer vacation began on the first of July—a few weeks after Sister Ōgin had punished Uruo and Marendo with the cat-o'-nine-tails. This summer was different from those in the past when the two boys spent their days tree climbing, playing catch, solving puzzles. All seventh graders were required to select seminars and attend them three hours daily in the morning for five days a week until the end of August. Uruo selected math for his summer study. The teacher gave her students plenty of homework. Uruo's daily schedule consisted of his kitchen work early in the morning, the math seminar until eleven o'clock, the preparation for dinner for all the St. Veronica population, free time until dinner, and then at eight o'clock he reported for dish-washing duty. Except when he played catch with Marendo behind the boys' dormitory, Uruo kept himself either in the main kitchen or in his room doing his math homework. Marendo complained that the English seminar he had chosen to take for the summer required excessive amounts of grammatically correct conversation exercises. His jaw got tired and was always tight: His teacher constantly pushed his students to speak properly, which required that the students paid constant attention to the exercises.

Uruo suspected Marendo had decided to take the English seminar because Yuri was in the class. Uruo toyed with the idea of joining them, to keep his eye on Marendo. But Uruo preferred numbers to words, even if his math was not as highly skilled as Marendo's. While taking the English seminar, Marendo continued with his tutoring. Initially he was assigned two students, but during the summer he was given five students to help. This meant he would get paid overtime. So would Uruo, by helping the kitchen in the afternoon for extra three hours.

One hot summer morning when cicadas were already shaking the air with their cacophonous chorus, Uruo saw Marendo skipping down the south slope toward the main office building when he should've been descending the north zigzag slope toward the school building. It only took a few seconds for Uruo to figure out what was going on with Marendo. Uruo decided to take the south slope down. On the last step, Uruo stopped and peeked out to see if Marendo was around. Sure enough, Marendo was leaning against the first of the pine trees that paralleled the pebbled path all the way to the iron gate. Marendo was looking straight ahead toward Mrs. Mori's nursing office. Then his face softened with a faint smile: Yuri exited from the nurse's office, passed by the entrance to the main office building, and came toward Marendo. She did not completely stop in front of Marendo. They exchanged a few words, which Uruo could not hear. Marendo touched Yuri's waist, and they headed for the pebbled path together toward the school building. They soon vanished out of Uruo's sight.

Uruo leaned against the concrete landslide barrier that ran along the slope. He thought of skipping the seminar that day, climbing up the camphor tree, and staying there all day. The view of Yuri and Marendo together implanted a sense of defeat in his heart, and the defeat soon turned into envy. At this point Uruo was unsure how he could get Yuri back from Marendo. He wanted to monopolize Yuri: he wanted her to be his—the image of her smooth cocoa-colored inner thighs had never left him. As he realized it now, he had not made his intention clear to her. That was why Marendo stepped in between Uruo and Yuri—he had no idea that Uruo liked her too. Uruo hoped Marendo's American face had not yet magnetized Yuri. Uruo's face suddenly turned hot, realizing how much he was indulging in this groundless assumption of Marendo's intentions, even spying on Marendo. Yuri and Marendo could have been going to school together as friends, just as Uruo had done with both Marendo and Yuri countless times before. Now defeat, envy, guilt, shame all jumbled up inside Uruo. Feeling insecure, he ascended up the slope—one step at a time.

Uruo ended up attending the math seminar, after all. But his focus was off the subject. Throughout the seminar, he fretted about what he had witnessed in the morning. In a way it was good that he let it bother him—an idea sparked in his brain, one that might help him pinpoint if Marendo and Yuri were serious about each other, or if they were just good friends. It became clear, also, that Uruo felt peeved because Yuri, despite her skin color, spoke with Marendo on equal terms—no hesitation, no affectation, no flattery. Marendo was a beautiful white boy: Uruo was aware of it. And, although Uruo denied it whenever this thought entered his mind, Uruo did admire Marendo's masculine beauty. But, to Uruo, a black girl should go out with a black boy—not with a handsome white boy. It irritated Uruo when Yuri treated him as if he were her little brother. He did not need a big sister.

At eleven o'clock when the math seminar was over, Uruo stopped by the English seminar room to see Marendo, who was just about to leave the classroom.

"You tutor today, don't you?" Uruo asked. "Why don't you meet me in the dish-washing room at two-fifteen?"

"Oh, why—something's up? Or is there a special treat?"

"Bring Inga and Yuri with you."

"I'd like that. They will be thrilled."

"Two-fifteen, then."

The main kitchen was quiet. It was too early for the head chef, Mr. Daigo, to start preparing for the day's dinner. Uruo mixed powdered agar and water, poured the mix into a frying pan, and simmered it until the mix began foaming. He then filled a flat aluminum container with the melted mix and gently inserted a thin bamboo separator to make small cubes. Normally he would put it in the refrigerator for three hours, but this time he put it in the freezer to speed up the process of coagulation. While the mix was hardening in the freezer, he sliced two medium size white peaches, put them in a ceramic bowl, and emptied a can of Mandarin oranges into another bowl. After placing the bowls in the refrigerator, he opened a bag of dried *azuki* beans, poured some into a pan and added water just enough to sink the beans evenly and let it boil. He then strained the boiling water, washed the cooked *azuki* beans under running water, and put the beans back into the pot. He had to watch the next step: the mixing of the softened beans with a small amount of water while stirring it and feeding more water until the beans became pasty. He added *san'ontō*—a light brown sugar—to the bean paste, and then mixed two ounces of *matcha*, and added some salt. The consistency of the bean paste felt slightly too soft, but Uruo knew the paste would get hard as it cooled. He spread the paste on a bamboo rice roller to let it cool evenly. He tasted a spoonful of it and decided the *azuki* paste came out just as he had thought it would. Uruo gave an affirmative grunt to the idea of mixing the intense green tea flavor the *matcha* with the *azuki* bean—not even Mr. Gen would have attempted to create something like this in his bakery.

Yuri tapped one of the kitchen windows with her fingers. Inga's dark face popped up by Yuri's. The sliding wooden door of the dish-washing room rattled; it was Marendo's habitual way of opening the door. Uruo took out from the freezer the aluminum container with coagulated cubed agar. When he shook the container side way, the cubed agar shook—which meant the timing for hardening agar was just right. To make his *anmitsu* snack, Uruo arranged the agar cubes, the *matcha-azuki* paste, a small amount of vanilla ice cream, with two slices of peach in each of four tin bowls, topping it with honey and a stemmed cherry. With the four bowls of *anmitsu* snack on a tray, Uruo took the tray to the dish-washing room.

"Snack time, guys." Uruo put the tray on the table by the door and unfolded three small rickety folding chairs that he had brought in from the main kitchen storage and placed against the wall by the table. Uruo served the *anmitsu* dish first to Inga, then to Yuri, and to Marendo. He avoided eye contact with all of them.

"Gosh, I've never had anything so fancy!" Inga said.

"Try it, Inga," Uruo said.

Yuri scooped a small amount of *anmitsu* paste and a few cubes of agar and tasted them together. She closed her eyes and moved her mouth with her lips closed. "The bean paste got a racy taste to it—something extra's in it, isn't there, Uruo?"

"Sure is. You'll have to figure it out for yourself."

"What a delicious snack!" Inga said, one corner of her lips white with ice cream, and her mouth full of *anmitsu*.

"Got more?" Marendo asked, mixing all the *anmitsu* ingredients.

"See, that's how you eat *anmitsu*." Uruo pointed to Marendo's tin bowl. "Sorry, I only made enough for one each."

"C'mon, Uruo. What did you do with the *azuki* paste?" Yuri said.

"I'm not telling you, Yuri. If you want to know, you will have to steal my secret recipe notebook."

"Where is it?"

"I'll ask Mr. Daigo." Marendo stuck his chest, proud that he came up with this idea.

"Mr. Daigo doesn't know," Uruo said, glaring at Marendo.

"I don't care who knows what. This is so good. When I graduate next April, I'm going to eat *azuki* paste every day."

"You won't get one like this," Yuri said.

Marendo was studying Inga's wound on her left cheek, now healed enough to no longer need its gauze dressing—his green eyes turned dark as if reliving the force of Sister Ogin's hand tearing the saw from his right hand at the crape myrtle tree that day.

Yuri suggested to Inga she should scoop ice cream, *azuki* paste, and agar cubes all at once and let them melt in her mouth.

Uruo ate the two slices of peach first, then mixed everything in the bowl including mandarin oranges and crammed a heap of *anmitsu* into his mouth.

"Here Inga, take half of my *anmitsu.*" The content of Yuri's bowl slid into Inga's bowl.

"Oh, you don't have to do that."

Yuri patted Inga's back. "Uruo will share with me." She dumped a small amount of left over in her bowl into Uruo's and dipped her spoon into his bowl which was now halfway filled. She let a scoop of melted *anmitsu* slide into her mouth. Then she winked at Uruo, her mouth moving in a small circle.

Uruo threw her a faint smile.

Marendo finished his share of *anmitsu*. Inga poured one-third of her *anmitsu* into Marendo's bowl.

"What's the matter with you, Eggplant? You haven't said much." Yuri leaned forward to face Marendo, her mouth full of the snack.

Marendo grimaced, then smiled at Yuri. "Good stuff." He seemed preoccupied with the taste of the *anmitsu*.

"I do have some leftover *azuki* paste in the kitchen. You guys want to help me finish it?" Uruo asked.

"Bring it in. I'll finish it," Marendo said, glancing at Inga.

Marendo's nonchalance toward Yuri caught Uruo by surprise. Uruo had been prepared to catch him ogling at Yuri. "All right."

As soon as he stepped out of the dish-washing room, Uruo came right back in and dove down onto the floor.

"Jesus." Marendo stopped eating.

Uruo abruptly squatted on the floor and, gesturing them to do the same, whispered: "Ōgin and three blonde hello-*san*. She's giving them a tour of the place."

"Is she going up the slope to your dorm?" Yuri asked. "That's her route, you know. Boys' dorm first. And then she will go down the north slope to the school and the church. Then she sees them off at the gate. Did she see you?"

"No. She was busy talking. I was afraid she might come this way." Uruo then looked at the long window on the other side of the room. "There they go." He pointed at the four women framed in the windowpane, ascending the zigzag steps.

The four children squatted near the table, packed close together like sardines in a can. Yuri clung on to Uruo's waist from behind, and Marendo cupped Yuri's breasts from behind.

Yuri turned around and stared at Marendo. Her slap across Marendo's face echoed in the room. "What are you doing!"

"Oh, God." Marendo's cheek was marked red with the trace of Yuri's fingers. "I am so sorry."

Uruo remained silent.

March 1967

THE FOUR aged cherry trees by the chapel blossomed like giant cotton candy. And, in the spring breeze, their petals swirled like snowflakes, gently landing on the ground and carpeting the chapel's front yard. At eleven-thirty in the morning that day, fourteen ninth graders—nine boys and five girls, Yuri and Inga included—had completed their graduation ceremony at St. Veronica's School.

Father Sainen selected Uruo to serve as the waiter for the graduation lunch held at the playground outside Sister Ōgin's executive suite. The table included Sister Ōgin at one end and Father Sainen at the other, nine boys on the left side and five girls and three teacher representatives on the right. A white cloth with silky luster covered this long table.

Uruo accepted this job because Father Sainen had offered him an over-time rate. This would raise his April income to eight hundred yen instead of the usual five hundred he earned working in the main kitchen. He liked the pleasant touch of the large and thick five-hundred-yen coin; but he preferred the sensation of holding in his palm five or more one-hundred-yen coins that were thinner and smaller. He liked, too, the soft shine of the one-hundred yen more so than the majestic golden glow of the five-hundred yen. The money he would have earned in the next two hours would fatten up his post-office savings—maybe he would be slightly richer than Marendo.

Since all nineteen guests would have the same menu, Uruo did not need to take individual orders. His job began when Mr. Daigo rolled in a metal cart with two large transparent plastic pitchers filled with sweetened iced tea. Mr. Daigo told Uruo that more iced tea had been made in case the guests might ask for seconds. Hot tea, too, Mr. Daigo said, was ready—especially for Sister Ōgin and Father Sainen who took delight in all things British. Mr. Daigo patted Uruo's back, then returned to the kitchen. Uruo stood a few steps away from the table.

"Let us pray," Father Sainen said. And the guests joined their hands.

Uruo rolled down his white shirt sleeves and buttoned them and bowed his head low. He only heard Father Sainen's muffled pitch, not the words of the prayer. Although his head was low, he was looking at Sister Ōgin's hands. They were white. They seemed as if made of pure, pristine marble. Those were the hands that threw Uruo into the holly bush when he had arrived at St. Veronica's. Now the bush's branches were sturdier and leaves were thicker than before. But the size had remained the same, like a bonsai tree—like a Chinese bound foot of ancient times.

Those hands had cut Inga's face. Uruo was certain Inga was happy to leave this place. In a year or two she would be dancing for the servicemen in khaki uniform, like her mother used to do years ago. Inga had told us her name would be "Black Rose." She would be a great hit—Uruo knew it because dancing was what she loved and that was all she was good at, just like how Uruo was a natural in the kitchen. Next year when he would leave St. Veronica's, he could be a fairly well accomplished cook. He did not think of himself going to senior high school and college after that.

Those same hands had whipped his back and almost crippled Marendo—he would remember that punishment until his last day on this earth. The only thing was that he had not figured out who had tied Marendo and him to the tree early that morning. They woke up to find their hands tied and both had been blindfolded during the night.

The night before the whipping, after the police officer and the juvenile department officer had driven Uruo and Marendo back to

St. Veronica's from Mitsukaidō, the two boys were confined in the guest lavatory by the reception room in the front part of the main office building. He remembered how long he felt the return trip was—so long that he had lost track of time. But these officers had been good to the boys. They allowed the boys to spend the car ride in silence without questioning them or scolding them. They had already been through enough.

When Uruo returned to the reality of the graduation lunch, Sister Ōgin's clear voice had replaced Father Sainen's, congratulating the graduating children, encouraging them to be self-reliant, self-assured, and worthwhile. They were, Sister Ōgin continued with her plastic enthusiasm, the children of God and they were to spread the Gospel like Christ's disciples had done.

Father Sainen nodded to Uruo, signaling that he should start serving. Uruo approached the metal cart, picked up a plastic pitcher, and poured iced tea into Sister Ōgin's glass first, then Father Sainen's, and the teacher representatives'. From there, he served all the girls before the boys.

Yuri suddenly raised her right hand—with her fingers bent elegantly and spaced just so, as if a petite flower arrangement placed in an alcove beneath an ancient scroll hung on a wall. She then snapped her fingers and spoke in a highly affected tone, with her lips puckered up: "Waiter, a glass of whisky on the rocks, please." Yuri raised her eyebrows at Uruo, her graceful hand suspended in space.

Father Sainen nearly spat his iced tea up. The teacher representatives could not hide their initial shock, then they all burst out laughing at the same time. All of them quietly covered their mouths with their hands, muting their laugh. Some of the children giggled watching those teacher representatives laugh. Controlling his hard laugh, Father Sainen glanced at Sister Ōgin. She pretended to look at no one, not laughing; then, turning to Yuri, she shook her head—as if to say: "Only you could get away with it, girl."

Five large sugar bowls, carved and lacquered in the Kamakura style, were lined up at regular intervals in the middle of the table.

These bowls made Uruo beam as he continued serving iced tea. Mr. Daigo was aware how the children loved the taste of sugar yet could not have it because it remained under strict ration at all times. Uruo loved sweets, and he could not imagine even one child who would refuse sugar—or anything sweet for that matter. Before tending the table, in the main kitchen, Uruo had thrown three tablespoons of the dark brown sugar into his mouth. The bowls of sugar were a gift from Mr. Daigo to the graduating children. Although the chief chef had never said anything to anyone, including Uruo, about this gift, Uruo knew Mr. Daigo had been preparing for it since the seven days of New Year's celebration had ended.

Returning to the metal cart to put the pitcher back there, Uruo caught sight of Inga's glass packed with sugar. She was stirring her iced tea slowly, so as not to make noise. The sugar swirled to the top of the iced tea, turning it to walnut from dark brown. Inga's glance met Uruo's. Inga's coquettish pretense signaled to Uruo that he had not seen her. Smiling, he quietly disappeared from the celebration scene.

A large cart with three tiers, like a medium-size mansion with three floors, carried fifteen dishes. Uruo handled this cart first. Then he brought out another cart one-third smaller than the first. A large grilled chicken leg, a steamed corncob with butter on the side, and two pieces of bread—each with a white cross imprinted on top of it, filled each celebration dish. In presenting a full plate per guest, he followed the same routine—Sister Ōgin first, Father Sainen second, the teacher representatives, the girls, and then the boys.

"Beautiful, aren't they?" The parallel lines of plates pleased Sister Ōgin. "You may use your fingers to have the chicken." She then cut up her chicken into pieces with her knife and fork.

Uruo looked at Sister Ōgin's clever hand movement and awed that she had used these western utensils for years while she lived in England. Uruo shifted his attention to Father Sainen. He too was adept at handling those strange eating utensils, though much more slowly than Sister Ōgin. But there was nothing strange about Father Sainen's slow stance: He was a man of composure.

Once Sister Ōgin gave permission to use their fingers to eat, the children quickly found out that they could use their fingers on all three items on their plates. Tension among the graduating children ebbed away. Uruo chortled at the thought of them eating their desserts with their fingers. Their voices mingled with the soft rustles of the young leaves surrounding the playground.

Each guest would have a mini *yōkan* with chestnut bits in it, two dried pineapple rings, and a cup of green tea. Uruo had prepared nineteen plates of desserts about two hours ago under Mr. Daigo's supervision. The chef had stressed that the arrangement of dessert on a plate must be pleasing to the eye.

Having served the dessert and green tea, Uruo stood behind the boys, his hands clasped behind his back. Inga and Yuri, as they were engrossed in their private conversation in whispers, had no idea Uruo was silently bidding farewell to them both.

St. Veronica's would be dead quiet without these two girls. They had been the Home's biggest clowns. They never changed from the time Uruo had first come to St Veronica's. Always the same, making other kids laugh.

Inga's sexy dance was St. Veronica's landmark. She had learned it well from her mom. Some people would say her kind of dance was for grownups. It occurred to him that Father Sainen had never said anything about her sexy dance. Uruo was eager to see her dance topless, with only a pair of tiny pink panties. Pink on jet-black skin—he sensed fever in his lower abdomen. She would look great on stage.

Even as Uruo fantasized about Inga's future, he could not accept that Yuri was also leaving the following week. He wished Yuri had failed two years before so that they could have been together in class. He never apprehended why, when she was talking to people and he was around, she would come over and put her long arm across his shoulders or coil around his arm and keep talking to them. She was warm, like a sister. But there was something more. So much more. Her touch was always magical: It made him want to get naked with her and get locked together with her, with that incredible trembling sensation she once gave him on the rooftop of the incineration building.

Suddenly, Uruo saw that Yuri and Inga were no longer talking. Their uninhibited chatty smiles had disappeared from their dark faces. Yuri looked puzzled about something Uruo could not imagine.

"Would you care for more green tea?" Uruo asked.

"No. No, thank you."

They returned to their dessert and green tea.

After the graduation lunch, Uruo was in the washing room behind the kitchen, cleaning up all the plates, glasses, and cups used during the lunch.

The door slid open slowly and Yuri slipped inside the room and closed the door behind her. She starred at Uruo for a moment.

"Yuri." Uruo put a plate back in the soap water and stood up. "Congratu—"

"Father Sainen was the one," Yuri whispered. "He tied you and Marendo to the tree that morning."

"No, he didn't." Uruo heaved. "How do you know?"

"Inga saw it all from the washroom window." She paused. "She was terrified she couldn't tell anyone—for a long time."

Yuri slipped out of the door.

Uruo stood in stunned silence. Soapy water dripped from his hands and onto the ground, slowly dribbling down the slanted floor and into the drain.

April 1967

Two weeks after the graduation ceremony, Inga left St. Veronica's Home to return to Yokosuka where her mother lived. Rumor had it that Inga's mother, suffering from chronic bronchitis and no longer even able to work as a janitor at the Seaside Cathedral in town, needed her daughter to take care of her.

Ten days following Inga's departure, Yuri left the Home to become a certified beautician. Father Sainen's older sister, a widow with no children, offered to provide Yuri with food and board while she trained at a cosmetology school in Shinbashi, Tokyo. In exchange, Yuri served the widow as a live-in housekeeper.

By early June all fourteen children who graduated that year had departed as indentured apprentices in their respective fields, assigned according to their aptitudes by the Prefectural Department of Welfare. Father Sainen and his office staff made detailed arrangements for every graduate—their clothes, pocket money of two thousand yen each to tie them over until their first paydays, and ensuring they had a place to live.

A year had gone by since and Uruo wondered if he would ever hear from Yuri again. No letters had come for him. Perhaps St. Veronica's policy of separating children from their families also extended to any unsupervised contact with the outside world.

Uruo wondered what he'd have to leave behind when he went out into the world like Yuri and Inga had before him.

"You think you'll go to America?" Uruo faced Marendo who

was doing his homework at his desk in the room he had shared with Uruo since the boys' dormitory had been built.

"No, I don't think about America, do you?"

"When I climb up my tree and see the ocean, I imagine America way beyond the horizon because our history teacher said so."

"He also told us about slavery."

"You think they will catch me and sell me as a slave if I went to America?"

"That was years and years ago, Uruo. But I hear the situation is still difficult."

"The same thing goes on here in our own country, too."

"'Our own country,' did you say?"

"Yeah. Isn't this our country?"

"Is it?"

"We were born and raised here, Marendo."

"But we don't look like them. Like those black people didn't look like white people. White people enslaved black people."

"What are you saying?"

"I'm saying we are not their kind. They don't think we belong with them. Look at us. We *are* different—you and me, other kids in the Home. They make it clear that we are outsiders, you know?"

"But they don't enslave us."

"But do they consider us their equals?"

"I guess not."

"What do you think they see us as?"

"Well, I guess the scum of the earth."

"Because we are mixed?"

"Not only that, Marendo." Uruo turned his chair to face Marendo. "We are born of men who fought against them—people who dropped A-bombs, of men who conquered them in 1945."

"I hear you. You've told me about your Aunt Kureo. She should have loved you as a nephew, but she still treated you like a monster."

"Much more than that. But it's good she doesn't have to dwell on it anymore. She passed away."

Marendo tapped his pencil against his unpainted veneer desk.

"We've gone through a lot together, brother." These words dribbled out of Marendo's lips as if they meant nothing.

"Yeah." Uruo tightened his lips and remained silent. Then he mumbled: "Pretending to love Sainen, the Judas Iscariot—the double-crosser. Am I learning to be a manipulator, at age fifteen, for survival?"

Marendo turned to the overgrown azalea tree outside the window in the courtyard of the dormitory. "When you shared with me what Yuri told you, my head went blank."

"I wanted to cry loud, so loud that the whole world could hear me. But I could not. I got numb all over. Then there was a big decision to make: whether to confront Sainen to get the truth and be shipped to reform school, or to feign ignorance and be one of his favorites."

"You went for the latter … you had to." Marendo shook his head. "So did I."

"You had to."

"Sainen might sense what we know?"

"Why do you ask?"

"No matter how good of an actor you are, inner changes show on the outside, Uruo. You can't hide the changes completely."

"So it's a contest of deceptions?"

"It looks that way."

"Just a few more weeks," Uruo said, sighing.

"Yeah."

Neither Uruo nor Marendo had ever understood why Sister Ōgin didn't send both of them to a juvenile reformatory after they had traveled to Mitsukaidō using the money they had stolen from the chapel's donation pot. Sister Ōgin punished them hard; but, since the day of the punishment, she had never mentioned their mischief or the punishment they had to endure as a result. In fact, she acted as if nothing had happened.

Uruo and Marendo had talked about this. It was out of the question that they could ask Father Sainen why they were still allowed to live in the Home after the punishment. They feared that Father Sainen might speak to Sister Ōgin, which would infuriate Sister Ōgin and she might whip them again. Marendo once said to Uruo that their next punishment might be a hanging—they would be suspended from tree branches and left there for a week with no food, no water: They would die. Every time Uruo thought of Marendo's story, he shivered with terror. Sister Ōgin's intentions were revealed a week before Uruo's departure from St. Veronica's.

Marendo graduated valedictorian, and Uruo was runner-up. They were honored together. It was, without a doubt, the most memorable event in Uruo's life. Strangely, though, he felt his honor should go to somebody else in his class because, for all those years, he hardly made any effort to study or to learn, even though he passed tests with high grades regardless of the subject. He preferred playing catch or rugby games with no official rules or cutting up vegetables and frying things in a huge wok that looked like a solar eclipse made flat on the electric stove.

Uruo enjoyed listening to Mr. Daigo talk about the apprenticeship he had entered when he was fifteen. Uruo would be captivated by his expressive voice just as much as the events he narrated. Mr. Daigo was a great storyteller, but was a teaser, too: He got a kick out of making Uruo shudder hearing about how to cook weird creatures from the sea like anglerfish, blowfish, and jellyfish. It was through days of casual conversations with Mr. Daigo that Uruo had learned the difference between Ginza tempura and Asakusa tempura, and then how to cook them in such ways that customers would taste the difference. Uruo liked the Asakusa tempura over the Ginza because the Asakusa's dressing was thicker than the Ginza's, which made the Asakusa much tastier and worthwhile eating. Mr. Daigo encouraged Uruo to use various materials to make tempura: sweet potatoes, bamboo shoots, vegetables—both in the Ginza and the Asakusa styles. One day Mr. Daigo reported to Father Sainen how creative Uruo's approach to tempura making was, and that his unique attributes be further developed under the mentorship of a professional chef.

Mr. Daigo's recommendation delighted Uruo. With no hesitation, Uruo accepted Father Sainen's offer to go to Tokyo and spend three years as an apprentice at Ibe Tempura in Asakusa. Mr. Daigo said Ibe Tempura, which went into business right after the war, was widely known in Tokyo for its traditional eighteenth-century tempura flavor. Uruo was further intrigued that Jingo Ibe, the owner of Ibe Tempura, was the only living person who knew how to cook this Tokyo specialty. Since he had lost all his family members during the Great Aerial Bombing of Tokyo in March 1945, Ibe was truly the only person who kept this culinary secret in his heart. This meant that upon his death the family secret would be gone. Uruo wanted Ibe's tempura secret. He wanted Ibe to bequeath it to him. Uruo sensed a great possibility in Father Sainen's suggestion and imagined his bright new future in Tokyo. His heart was set on his new life in Asakusa that was to start in mid-April.

Contrary to Uruo's aspiration for his new life in Asakusa, something seemed to be going on in Marendo's head—he had been brooding since their graduation in mid-March. When he was trying to figure out things that bothered him, or was focusing on solving some math problems, Marendo always became distant, paying no attention to his surroundings. Sometimes he would ignore his dormitory mates, including Uruo. When Marendo was distant like this, Uruo left him alone. Marendo would come back to himself sooner or later, when he was ready.

This time Marendo remained in his shell longer than usual. Uruo was taken by surprise when Marendo came into the dish-washing room after eight o'clock in the evening and sat on a low stepladder by the table. Uruo had finished scrubbing two large cauldrons and the wok.

The hot water hose he used for scrubbing was thick; it was cumbersome to coil it up. "What brings you here?" Uruo said, hanging the coiled hose on an iron stake sticking out of the brick wall.

"I wanted to warm my feet." Marendo rubbed his sandaled feet.

"Oh?"

"I'm lying."

"Spit it out."

Marendo sighed, gesturing for Uruo to come over to the table.

Uruo came over and, leaning against the edge of the table, pulled out a piece of ripped rag from his pant pocket and wiped his wet feet clean. He then put his black canvas shoes on and folded his arms, facing Marendo.

"Father Sainen said he and Sister Ōgin sent recommendations to the admission committee of International High School in Yokohama."

"The one with no entrance exams?"

"Right. Because IHS is run by the Association of American Episcopal Churches. Your junior-high transcript and recommendations are what they look at."

"You got accepted?"

Marendo nodded, regretfully.

"And did you say yes to Father Sainen?"

"No. I don't know if I can."

"Why?" Uruo squatted on the floor and looked up at Marendo's frowning face. "You'd be an idiot not to. You know that?"

"How can I? I learned English just like you did at school. But I don't speak it."

"You said it's an international school. There will be students from non-English speaking countries. Right?"

"Yeah, but …"

"Knowing you, you'll master the language as soon as you hear it—a hands-down victory for you." Uruo stood up.

Uruo grabbed Marendo's arm and said, "Let's go to the kitchen. I've got some goodies for you."

In the kitchen, Uruo went straight to the freezer that the Red Cross had donated to the Home a few years back when Uruo had begun his kitchen duty. Uruo opened the freezer, took out a square pan, then placed it on the cooking counter, and opened the lid.

A mist of dry, icy air shot out of the freezer. Marendo gently pushed it shut.

"These are the side dishes for the dinner tomorrow for the staff members. Kids have a different menu. I made these tempura a few hours ago. Mr. Daigo lets me cook now. I've made some extras. So, here, take whatever two pieces you want."

"No wonder you're getting big all over." Marendo chose a string bean and a good-sized clam.

Uruo warmed them in a miniature frying pan until the oil sputtered out. "Okay, they are ready for you."

Marendo ate the string bean first. "You're a pro cook already." He raved about the clam.

Uruo watched Marendo move his jaws like a cow, never wanting to miss even one ounce of an ingredient in Uruo's tempura. At that moment Uruo saw Marendo returning to the child he once was, the only boy who spoke to him on his first night at the Home. Uruo remembered thinking: He is fearless. And the next morning, he walked over to school with this fearless boy. That was seven years ago, seven long years in which he had been separated from his home and his family. Uruo had known Marendo for almost half of his life. He wasn't eager to lose him.

Tuesday, April 18, 1967 arrived sooner than Uruo had expected.

He could barely sleep the night before. Nervous energy kept him awake and fitful until morning. Expectation, exultation, anticipation, fright, self-doubt—all of these eddied in chaos. One minute he would want to embrace the whole world celebrating his independence, the opportunity to grow as a man, on his own. Yet the next minute he would shut out all this aspiration, tormented by the color of his skin. Then the images of Yuri and Inga drifted into his thoughts. They were always laughing about something, or somebody. They made fun of each other, too—Yuri teasing Inga about her inflated chest, and Inga picking on Yuri's flat butt that had a purple mole on the left side. Since they departed St. Veronica's a year ago, neither had come back to visit.

Uruo had an idea how Yuri would handle the condescending stares, the ostracizing remarks, and the dismissive attitudes against her because of her dark skin. Her impromptu wit would stir and make her offenders laugh. What about Inga? Uruo wasn't sure what her tactics would be. She couldn't go around extending her long shapely arms like Marilyn Monroe, shaking her shoulders and oversize breasts at those who would spit at her.

Their images vanished from his mind.

Only a vacuum remained.

The morning sky, now a pale orange light replacing the purple clouds dotted with vanishing stars, foretold a day of warmth and radiance. Uruo woke up from a light sleep and brushed his teeth and washed his face. The ice-cold water penetrated his face and through his skull. By the time he put on his casual clothes, he was wide awake. He quietly closed the dormitory's entrance door. And, like a sandpiper hopping across the seashore, he danced the zigzag slopes down to the kitchen, to help Mr. Daigo for the last time.

At ten o'clock, dressed in a pair of black jeans, a white button-down dress shirt, and a black V-neck sweater, Uruo stood in front of the main office building, waiting for Father Sainen who would accompany him to Asakusa, Tokyo as was required by the federal welfare law. The rucksack felt cumbersome on his back. Miss Hogi, the house mother of the boys' dormitory, had packed for him three sets of undershirts and underwear, two pairs of old pants, three polo shirts, an old white-and-blue striped sweater, and a winter jacket. But these clothes should not have weighed this much. He dropped the sack on the grass and opened it to see what else was in it. He slid his hand underneath the stack of clothes, grabbed what felt like a book. He pulled it out of the sack. It was a copy of the book entitled *Traditional Japanese Cuisine: 1600~1900*. Miss Hogi had inscribed a message: "Good luck on your journey and Godspeed!" He gently laid the book between two soft undershirts and zipped up the sack.

Marendo joined Uruo and Father Sainen at the gray boulder by the iron gate. Three of them marched out of the gate. Father Sainen was admiring the cream-colored trees germinating behind the train station. The distance between the Home's gate and the train station required only a two-minute walk. But, for Uruo, it seemed to take forever. Uruo and Marendo exchanged no words.

At the Chinosaki train station, Father Sainen and Uruo passed the ticket gate and entered the platform. Marendo leaned on the lattice that separated the platform from the waiting area.

Uruo turned around. And, walking backward, he waved to Marendo.

"Uruo!" Marendo jumped over the lattice, ran to Uruo and hugged him. Uruo hugged Marendo, tight.

"I wish you could stay with me here in Chinosaki."

"Tokyo is waiting for me, Marendo," Uruo whispered. "I want my own life."

The bell shrieked five times to signal the departure of the train.

They let go of each other. Uruo hurried into the passenger car.

The train pushed forward.

Marendo watched the brown face sticking out of the passenger car's window recede into the distance. The face turned into a dot. And the horizon engulfed the last passenger car.

PART 03

Asakusa

1967 ~ 1972

October 1967

THIRTEEN STALL blocks flanked Nakamise Street: five on the west side, eight on the east side. Ibe's Tempura occupied one-third of the second stall block on the east side. On the north end of Nakamise Street, and beyond Hōzō Gate, reigned the main hall of Sensō-ji. And on the south end prevailed Kaminari Gate with a set of four double-pairs of orange-red pillars on each side supporting the gate. Between the pillars hung a colossal lantern which, as Uruo recalled from his early days in Asakusa, Mr. Jingo Ibe said he had never seen lit since its installation in 1960.

Ibe owned a two-story house behind his tempura stall, separated by a dirt alley parallel to the east side of the stall blocks. Until the American air raids destroyed Asakusa in 1945, his family had owned a large estate on the same lot. The destruction left only a small segment of what used to be a stone wall on the south side of the house. With this wall as a corner stone, Ibe had built his two-story house. The house had weathered hurricanes, earthquakes, rainstorms, blizzards for the past twenty-some years. Now it stood solid, surrounded by new buildings. Ibe had said to Uruo that he used to rent the second floor of the house to some young newly-weds but that arrangement lasted only for four years. The couple bought their own house in the residential town of Kunitachi, twenty-one miles west of Asakusa. Since then, until he hired Uruo as his apprentice six months before, Ibe had lived alone on the first floor of this house.

Now Uruo occupied one half of the second floor—an eight-*tatami* room. The other room remained vacant. A set of four sliding screens divided the two rooms, but Uruo kept these screens open. The south end of the vacant room displayed a large Chinese painting spread over the four sliding screens that encased the *futon* storage. The painting exhibited overlapping mountain ridges, each standing at a different height. At the lower right corner of the third screen from the left end was a crane, with his wing stretched wide, about to land. The crane's red cap shone against the hazy greenish-gray mountains. Sometimes Uruo would sit in the middle of his room, cross-legged, and gaze at this screen painting and let himself be drawn into magical serenity of the mountains across the screens.

When the sun was out, Uruo kept the glass doors open. He returned to his room from the shop at ten o'clock at night. The noise coming from the town below and the aroma of food still floating in the night air tingled his skin. He was content lying spread-eagle on the *tatami* mats, sucking in the raw smell of woven rush grass that covered the mats, and reflecting upon the faces of those stall keepers in the neighboring stalls around Ibe's Tempura that crossed his memory. All day long, with a vigor Uruo had never known, those stall keepers appealed to tourists who flooded Nakamise Street heading for Sensō-ji and returning to Kaminari Gate.

The number of foreign tourists whose glances Uruo had met since his first day at the Ibe's stall was, he was certain, greater than the total number of all the foreigners he had come across in the entire fifteen years of his life before he came to Asakusa. In Mitsukaidō and in Chinosaki, Uruo was like a deformed pumpkin displayed on a vendor's stand which locals stared at, picked up, smelled, and dumped back on the stand. In Asakusa, those countless chiseled white faces with golden hair, those with dark skin—some with straight noses and socketed eyes too, and those Asian faces with strange lip movements uttering unfamiliar sounds captivated Uruo. His thoughts returned to the camphor tree with the gnarl that canopied the incineration building in St. Veronica's Home, to the expanse of blue waters that had alluded to something out there beyond the horizon.

Those foreign tourists on Nakamise Street must have come from somewhere beyond the horizon that used to fascinate him. It must be his karma that their paths would cross, he surmised. Exhilaration mixed with anticipation whirled behind his eyes.

Since Uruo began serving his own creation, a special mixed tempura, Ibe's Tempura stall had turned into a stopping point for those tourists visiting Nakamise Street. Uruo served his tempura from twelve noon to one o'clock in the afternoon. Uruo would mince prawns, carrots, broccoli, ginger, and green onions, and mix them in a bowl. Next, he scooped the raw mix with a large slotted spoon and dipped the mix into a tempura dressing containing starch, eggs, a minuscule amount of garlic, and a dash of chili powder. He then stir-fried the scoop in a wok with vegetable oil for about two minutes—letting his customers see how the dressed raw materials would transform into vivid gold in the spluttering oil. And he sold two pieces of tempura as a set for three hundred yen—a price higher than usual. Despite this high price, Nakamise tourists raved about the croquette-like taste of his unique tempura.

The rest of the day he spent cutting up raw materials in large chunks, lining them up on square pans and placing them at a narrow window-like shelf for Ibe to pick up from the other side of the shelf. Ibe dipped the raw material one at a time into a bowl of dressing mixture—the family culinary secret—and stir-fried it in the wok. He then put the tempura on a paper plate and received the payment.

One day a wrestler-like foreign tourist stuck his head between shop curtains hung from the eaves and requested in Japanese that was heavily accented, "I'd like three plates of Uruo fusions." Uruo gazed at the wrestler's red hair covering his massive head while deciphering what he meant by "Uruo fusion." Through Ibe, Uruo had learned the meaning of the English word "fusion" to mean a combination of things, which, Ibe added, had become a trendy word in Tokyo, recently imported from America. He quickly saw that the red-haired giant meant "Uruo's fusion tempura." Someone must have named his tempura.

But Ibe did not allow "Uruo fusion" to appear on his official signboard.

"Why you don't want it on our menu?" Uruo asked.

"You don't speak to your master like that, boy."

"But …"

"Yes?" A pair of bright and tender eyes shone against his wrinkled stern face.

"You gave me permission to sell my tempura for one hour a day. People like it. They know about it. They pay for it."

"So?"

"Our menu should have 'Uruo fusion,' Mr. Ibe."

"Not yet. Have you forgotten your probationary period? You aren't a full employee yet."

"No, sir. I haven't forgotten it. But I felt good enough to talk to you about my ideas."

"Our signboard should always read 'Ibe's Tempura.' I owe it to my ancestors. And to the people who visit Nakamise Street, since my shop is now an Asakusa landmark. Nothing extra on the signboard. Nothing special on the menu. Understood?"

"Yes, sir."

"Finish your probation—three more weeks."

"Yes, sir."

An invisible smile played about Ibe's lips that resembled an unzipped coin purse.

It stirred Uruo's curiosity that Ibe had never said anything about his skin color. Ibe made no big deal of a black boy living on the second floor of his house. Once in a blue moon, he had called Uruo "son." But what would Ibe call him when he turned twenty years old and celebrated the Coming-of-Age Day and he was no longer a kid? Uruo looked forward to this day.

Uruo knew those stall-keepers gossiped about Ibe having Uruo as his apprentice. Ibe couldn't care less. Once, Uruo overheard a middle-aged woman, whom the Nakamise stallers called "Miwa," whispering to Ibe about Uruo. Miwa sold cheap *kimono* and *yukata* in the third stall block on the west side of the street. Uruo saw her every day, but she never said anything. She stared at Uruo. Miwa was saying to Ibe she thought Uruo was an American Negro with a weird smell. Ibe laughed in her face and said: "He is a Lebanese exchange student, making some pocket money. He wants to travel Kyushu next spring." And Ibe kept on cooking his tempura. Uruo could not believe what he heard. His body got hot. His stomach groaned and the noise traveled across his lower belly: it felt like several *ume* seeds were bumping into each other, trying to find an exit. Ibe never mentioned a word about the Lebanese boy story he had made up.

The remaining three weeks passed by fast. Uruo's probation period ended in late October of that year. That he was now Ibe's full employee did not change anything much. Uruo still got up at four-thirty in the morning, swept all the *tatami* rooms including Ibe's, and swabbed down wooden passageways on both floors. He then sprinkled water and scattered salt across the dirt alley between the house and Ibe's stall—to protect them from calamity and to chase away evil night spirits. He then received deliveries from the Chikuji Fish Market: prawns, shrimp, congers, whitebait, goby, and many more. While Uruo was doing his chores, Ibe cooked a small amount of rice for Uruo and himself for breakfast. Ibe placed the first bowl of rice in front of the house altar built on the wall of a four-*tatami* sitting area behind the kitchen. He and Uruo stood in front of the altar and, each joining his hands, they prayed. Uruo was certain Ibe had something to pray for. He himself had nothing to pray for to Ibe's ancestors. He followed Ibe's gestures while his brain was already tasting Ibe's fluffy white rice, sweet and sticky in his mouth. A bowl of miso soup and a piece of leftover fish, also. Leftovers that had refrigerated overnight, and had just been warmed up, had a seasoned taste different from when they were made fresh.

Ibe's prayer lasted long. At last Ibe bowed to the altar, which meant the end of his prayer. Uruo, too, bowed, with no reason.

"I thought about adding 'Uruo's fusion' to the menu," Ibe said one day after the prayer. "I am unable to do it at this point. My ancestors' tradition must continue."

Uruo stopped pushing rice into his mouth with his chopsticks, removed the rice bowl from his mouth on to the table, frowning. "My probation is over now, sir."

"Who owns the business here, boy?"

"The fusion brings money, Mr. Ibe."

"You don't have to tell me that. Don't you forget your position here—Apprentice. And apprentices don't make decisions."

The realization that he was looking at his superior who could lie with composure like Father Sainen stunned Uruo. He could not swallow the ball of rice stuck in his throat. The miso soup he just gulped pressured the rice down, forcing his tube to open.

September 1968

WHEN HE first arrived at Ibe's house the previous spring, Uruo paid no attention to a footbath cubicle that had been built outside Ibe's kitchen. The kitchen water line and the footbath water line forked from the main plumbing system in the kitchen. The cubicle measured three feet by five feet. The shorter side attached to the outer wall of the kitchen. In front of the kitchen wall, and inside the cubicle, stood a three-foot concrete cylinder, with a rusted water faucet sticking out of it, facing east toward the backyard. The bamboo lattice, about four feet high, enclosed the cubicles, except the center of the south end that was kept open. Six small stepping-stones connected this opening and the entrance to the kitchen.

Ibe brought this footbath to Uruo's attention one day. He said, "You can use the footbath in the back anytime you want. I had it built years ago. Never used it." As if expecting Uruo's question, Ibe continued: "There is a public bath near Sumida River. That's where I go. Only five minutes from here."

Uruo had been there already. That was why he washed himself in the kitchen. Uruo rebutted Ibe's casual remark. "Kitchen sink's easier and faster than a public bath for me."

"All right, boy." This was all Ibe said, and he never mentioned it again.

Since that day, Uruo had tested the water faucet in the footbath cubicle several times, turning the handle in both directions to see how well it could control the flow of the water. Sometimes he touched the bamboo lattice with his fingers to see how solid the bamboo was after twenty-some years. Other times, he gazed at the precise workmanship of the brick floor, peeling off with his foot the moss spreading over the bricks like dark-green depths of ocean down on a map. His debate went on—the kitchen water could be boiled, but the process was cumbersome; the footbath water could run strong, but the temperature remained cold. One advantage in using the footbath was that he could get naked, and that he could wash himself without stopping to boil a few more potfuls of water. Yet, to do this, he would need a bowl to contain water and a stool to sit on while washing himself.

Uruo asked Ibe if he could buy a plastic water bowl and a wooden stool and pay from his salary.

"Good decision," Ibe said. "But … before you get those things …" Ibe folded his arms as if he was chilly. The windless autumn air was fresh. Ibe faced the northeast corner of the backyard. "Let me see if I have something in the storehouse there."

The old storehouse stirred Uruo's curiosity: its brown dirt walls, each side partitioned by two thick vertical beams and two equally sturdy horizontal beams under the tile-covered slanting roof, the ornamental tile of a devil's head with its mouth open attached to each ridge-end, and its entrance that appeared to have never opened.

"Come with me."

The ominous exterior of the storehouse, dark and reticent, stiffened Uruo. He followed Ibe.

The lock loosened as Ibe undid the two crisscrossed iron plates attached to the door. The door opened outward with no squeaking, and a red pine inner door stood before them. Ibe repeated the same unlocking motion with two wooden blocks at the lower left corner of the door. The red pine door opened inward, and Ibe pushed it further to find an electric switch on the left wall.

A pungent woody aroma ushered Uruo in. The inside panels, the beams, the staircase to the mezzanine floor—all emerged awe-inspiring. The spaciousness of the interior surprised Uruo. Ibe's possessions stored here seemed sparse.

"I knew I had it somewhere in here," Ibe said. He was looking at a large earthenware pot about two-and-half feet in height and eight feet in circumference. "Use this pot. Put it under the faucet and let the water run all the time. It looks like I have no stool, though."

"That's okay, sir. I can wash myself standing up." Uruo's eyes brightened as he shared with Ibe his new idea. "I see a pail with a handle up there, on the third shelf. May I use it, too?"

"Excellent."

As Uruo stretched on his toes to reach the pail, the aroma of cypress brushed his face. He studied the pail as if it were an antique. The grains, looking like miniature galaxies, patterned the pail.

"My uncle made it long time ago," Ibe said. "He died in the war."

Uruo stood still. "I'm sorry," he murmured.

"I want you to use it. My uncle would like that very much."

Back in the mid-May of that year, when Asakusa was still new to him, Uruo used to stroll the town after ten o'clock at night when he had closed the tempura stall. It was during his nightly stroll when Uruo came across Sentō Niji—a public bath with a faded, rainbow-colored awning. He first headed south on Nakamise, then crossed Hirokōji Street which ran east and west, and kept on going south a block. Niji stood at the end of this block, its frontal view resembling a Shinto shrine. Its rugged brick chimney shot up into the night sky, giving an illusion that it had been grafted into the shrine structure. A single *hiragana* character meaning "hot water" embroidered on the leftmost square shop-curtains hanging from the lintel of the entrance, identified the building as a public bath.

Uruo crossed the street and stood on the pavement opposite the Niji bathhouse. The black ridge-end tiles on the rooftop, each with a devil's mask with a pair of horns and fanged mouth, felt like they could stab him in the eye. They resembled the ones that ornated Ibe's storehouse in his backyard. His grandmother would say those devils were the protectors of the town. He was not sure whether to believe this legend or not.

A woman, hefty around her hips and with a round yellow washbowl held under her arm, came out and flapped the middle curtain, but then was quickly blinded by the same curtain flapping back at her face. She stumbled against the door rail, leaving her left wooden clogs behind, which pitched her forward. But she caught herself in time. She cursed the doorsill, picked up the clog, then slipped her small foot into it, and adjusted the clog's strap with her right fingers. She straightened her back and marched toward the intersection at the end of the block and turned west. Her washbowl looked as small as a rice bowl.

Then something clicked in his brain: If the bath is co-ed, he might be bathing with women. What if he had to bath with the plump washbowl lady? He would surely have bathed with Yuri. He had not forgotten Yuri's tight breast pressed against his side. Her runner's thighs, that he glimpsed when she lay on her stomach to watch the snake down on the ground, sent him to a galaxy unknown to him back then. Since that first ecstasy, he didn't know how many nights he had wet dreams and he devoured every one of those dreams. Soon after, he even learned to reproduce a similar sensation by using his own hands during those few times he was alone at St. Veronica's. Uruo never resisted these urges and felt no guilt about enjoying them.

But when he was younger, he was told he should never touch his own penis for pleasure. Grownups at St. Veronica's Home insisted that it was a sin to touch it.

At St. Veronica's, the girls and the boys bathed together until they had finished fourth grade. After that point, the girls bathed on Tuesdays and Fridays, and the boys on Mondays and Thursdays. The children formed small groups, some of three, others of four—each occupying the bath for fifteen minutes. On Mondays and Thursdays, at six-thirty in the evening when the boys trickled into the bath, Miss Hogi—the oldest boys' house mother—would come into the bath and promptly remove her blouse, slip, and skirt.

"Okay, boys. Time to scrub yourselves clean—real clean." This was her arrival call.

The boys giggled at Miss Hogi's cream-colored bra and matching underwear that perfectly enveloped her fleshy hips. She ignored their curious stares, particularly the ones focused on her lower belly where a slight mound could be visible through her panties.

"Plenty of soap, boys. Clean your behind and front. Make sure to pull back your little foreskins and wash there, too."

Her gentle command stopped their giggling and steered them right back to washing themselves. She scrubbed one boy at a time with a soapy loofah and then rinsed the soap off his back clean with hot water that was reserved in an oval wooden tub at the corner of the bath.

"Now, the sulfur bath. Jump in." She liked to pat their shapeless little buttocks and push them toward the largest rectangular tub of yellow sulfurous hot water that could hold seven to eight children.

Uruo and Marendo always made sure they were together in a group due for bathing at seven-thirty in the evening. By this time the temperature in the room would have risen and the steam would have filled the place from the concrete floor covered with slatted drainboards to the ceiling.

When it first happened, the time was about seven-thirty and the bath was full of steam, also. Both Uruo and Marendo were ten years old. Marendo stripped himself of all clothes and threw them in a cubicle in the changing area outside the bath. He dashed into the bath. But in the next moment he was right back in the changing area, standing still in front of Uruo, hiding his penis with his hands that looked larger than any other part of his slender body.

"What?"

"Miss Hogi."

"What about her …? Oh, shit—you're half hard." Uruo broadcasted.

"Shush!"

Uruo's high-pitched laugh fueled Marendo's blush.

Taking his time, Uruo folded his boxer shorts in four and put them on top of his white undershirt that laid on top of a pair of faded jeans. "Okay, let's go in and see what Miss Hogi's up to."

Uruo froze. In the middle of the thick steam was a blurry shape of Miss Hogi, stark naked, scrubbing a boy's bony back with a loofah. Uruo looked to Marendo who, in turn, bulged his eyes at him and nodded. Uruo covered his front with a hand towel.

"Are you boys coming in, or what?" Miss Hogi yelled.

Marendo disappeared into the steam first, detouring Miss Hogi. Uruo followed. They sat on two empty stools in front of the sulfurate hot tub and, as if mirroring each other, soaped their hand towels. Uruo's lower abdomen kept twitching as he sneaked a look at Marendo staring at Miss Hogi's left breast, her right breast, then her dark area below her sunken navel.

The following day Marendo told Uruo that the bath had gotten so hot that Miss Hogi decided to do away with her bra and panties and bathed with her boys. Uruo and Marendo, at once, made their decision to bathe at seven-thirty when Miss Hogi would be in her bare skin. Both boys agreed that Miss Hogi must have enjoyed bathing with her boys. After this incident, on every bathing day, Marendo was half hard in the bath; and Uruo's lower abdomen never stopped twitching while his lips remained tightly zipped.

Sentō Niji, seen from where Uruo was standing and reminiscing about Miss Hogi and Marendo, seemed to quiver in the heat haze coming out of the bathing area inside. A massive pillar of black smoke kept pushing itself out of the brick chimney high into the starless night sky. With it the smell of live coals pervaded the southern city block.

Uruo traversed Nakamise back to Sentō Niji. In the foyer behind the three rectangular curtains, he removed his shoes, put them in a shoe cupboard, and took three steps up into the changing room with wooden floor. To his right side was a windowed reception area where a young woman in her early twenties with a high ponytail was counting coins at her desk.

She looked up. Her left eyelash spasmed. "Pardon me. Do you speak—"

"Yes, ma'am, I do," Uruo said. "Is this *sentō* a co-ed?"

"No. The female section is to your left, and the male section to your right."

"And the fee?"

"Fifty yen."

She took a fifty-yen coin from Uruo without looking at him and, in return, handed him a bath towel, a hand towel, a mini soap, and a locker key that read 0-5-8. "When you are finished, deposit the towels in a slot on the right side before you open the sliding door back into the changing room. You may discard the soap. The key must be returned to me."

"Yes, ma'am."

She smiled, but she was looking somewhere beyond Uruo's left shoulder. "You must have studied the language before you came to Japan. Such high proficiency."

"I was born here."

"Oh, I had no idea, because you look so different ..." The woman stuttered. "I mean—"

"May I?" Uruo pointed his index finger toward the men's bath.

"Please."

Uruo slid the frosted glass door open into the changing area and closed it behind him. The locker with the key tag 0-5-8 was easy to find because its yellowish-beige color stood out among all other lockers that were gray. When he unlocked the small metal door, a clean scent wafted out. He peeked into the dark cubicle for more of this flowery aroma, though he did not know what flower would have such a strong fragrance that would draw and repel at the same time. He remembered a similar smell—a fragrance of high society—when he, on the way to Sumida River, passed by the main entrance of Matsuya Department Store three blocks east of

Nakamise Street. Although he liked the high society smell, he favored the sweaty smell of his own armpits and groin.

As he removed his clothes, he folded them one by one and stacked them in the locker. He peeled his hardened black socks off his feet, smelled them, and hung the pair on the hook screwed into the left side of the cubicle. The stink of his acid and oil at once drove the fragrance of high society out.

A loud laugh, perhaps of three or four men soaking in the bath, penetrated the wooden sliding doors that separated the bath from the changing room.

Uruo stood naked, facing the sliding doors, the hand towel covering his groin. The men's laughter and their yakking noises pricked Uruo's walnut skin. Hot pain surfaced from deep inside and spread up toward his shoulders and neck where whipping scars remained. He backed away from the door, but his right hand had already pushed the door leftward.

The men's noise broke off. Beyond the curtain of steam were four rugged, stocky faces—all tanned. One had a stubby beard, two of them had made their hand towels into headbands around their crew cuts, and the remaining one was bold, soaking himself right up to the nose, his stare firmly fixed on Uruo's well-defined broad chest and tight abdomen. From their appearances, Uruo surmised that they were laborers.

From the stacks of wooden stools and pails, Uruo took one of each, sat on the stool and filled the pail with hot water. The mini soap foamed well. Although his back faced the four laborers soaking in the large bathtub, Uruo could sense their whispers punctuated by silence of observation. They were all clustered at the left corner of the tub away from the faucet.

"Where are you from?" A throaty pitch.

Uruo ignored it and began scrubbing himself with the hand towel.

"Hey, you. He's talking to you," came another voice.

Uruo turned to the voices. "Excuse me?"

"I said, where are you from? Ethiopia? Nigeria?"

"I was born here."

"You sure don't have skin like ours."

They were back to whispering.

"Nobody will believe you," the throaty voice said, mockingly.

"I was born in Mitsukaidō,"

"Mitsukaidō?" one of the crew cuts said, in a high pitch. "We have a little black mouse from a countryside. How did you get here in Asakusa?"

"Mommy carried you on her back?"

"What about daddy? A black giant with a gigantic dick?"

All four burst out laughing.

Uruo threw hot water over his head and frothed up the soap with his fingers. He listened to the noise his fingers made as they scratched greasy dust off his scalp. Then he was scrubbing his right arm hard until it felt irritated and raw. Tears welled his eyes, but at first he did not realize why he was crying. Then it came back to him: the *kappa* at the Mitsukaidō pond. He instinctively touched his right thigh—there was no urine smell this time. The soap painted him white.

The rinsing was easy. The Niji custodian, Uruo supposed, must have kept feeding coals into the boiler in the backroom—the temperature of the hot water was so high that the heat would seep into the skin and circulate through the body, even to the tip of the toes. Uruo sat on the edge of the large tub, diagonal from where the four laborers gathered. He slipped into the hot water and soaked himself up to the neck, turning his back on them. He wrung the hand towel and put it on top of his head.

With the splash of the hot water, the stubby one abruptly got out of the tub and dried himself.

Uruo turned around to face them. His pupils expanded. He caught them sending quick eye signals among one another.

The hairless one and the two crew cuts followed the stubby toward a door with the sign "Customer Services."

The hot water settled motionless. Uruo's gaze glided over the glass-like water surface. He then paddled the water with his arm, drawing a horizontal half circle underwater. The water came alive, rippling in a leisurely pace. Breast-stroking, he rode the ripples, touched the other end of the tub where the four laborers had clustered, and without splash crawled back to the corner where he had first soaked himself.

The speaker discharged a sharp metallic monotone. It penetrated Uruo's brain from his left ear and exited out his right. An announcement followed: "In five minutes, the hot water in the men's bath will be refreshed. All customers are invited to the second floor for cold drinks and snacks. We apologize for the inconvenience."

Three large bubbles made rumbling noises one after the other, then ruptured. Below the faucet, the hot water was now swirling with a gargling sound, the level of the hot water in the bathtub visibly lowering. Along with the disappearing hot water, Uruo lowered himself in the tub so that his whole body would still be covered with the warmth of the water. But it did not last—the tub was nearly empty. Those laborers must have protested that the customers would deserve clean hot water, not stained by the filth of a black boy. Uruo needed no proof to know what had happened.

Uruo got out of the gargling tub and unhooked his bath towel to dry himself. When he returned his locker key to the receptionist, his glance collided with the stubby laborer. He was standing in the customer services office with the other three, all half-naked with their bath towels around their waists.

The night air perked up Uruo. Even the chemical smell of the live coals seemed agreeable to him. He looked up at the brick chimney. Tiny golden sparks, like lighting bugs, spurted out, encircling the soot. He attempted to count the sparks but stopped—they flew away too fast.

It occurred to Uruo that Ibe's kitchen could be his private bath after all.

May 1969

"OH, YOU'RE from Ibe's! Fantastic!" A potbellied middle-aged man with a broad face praised Uruo, patting the left lapel of his kimono-style livery coat that read "Ibe's Tempura." The man wore the same livery coat. On his back were three *kanji* characters written in white that read "Nakamise," like Uruo's.

Uruo had not met this man. But the man knew Ibe's Tempura. "I'm Uruo Yusa—working for Ibe."

"I know. Most of the Nakamise group do. You must be honored Ibe hired you."

"Thank you. Mr. Ibe is a great mentor for me."

"You have been with Ibe for a while now, haven't you?"

"Yes. A little over two years."

"Let me tell you, young man, your 'fusion' is a real seller. Ibe is a silent man, but he is very much pleased with your business acumen. I know this, because we drink together from time to time and we talk. He is truly a Nakamise treasure. He could be a national treasure if he lives long enough." The man emphasized the words "national treasure" with a higher pitch. The man traced Uruo's gentle smile and linked it to the girl behind his lumber-like arm. "Oh, this is my daughter, Rika. She's carrying a portable shrine today. Such a tomboy."

"Hi, Uruo," the girl said. "You're carrying one, too. Right?"

Her black hair in a knot on top of her head, braced by a yellow headband, brought her face forward into relief—a pair of thick eyebrows shaped like two mountains with smooth slopes extending opposite directions, a pair of large black pupils gripping Uruo's gaze, thin and long lips, and a crescent jaw line.

"You two know each other?"

"Sort of."

"Every time she comes to the shop, she eats three orders of fusion tempura."

"No, I do not." Clinging on to her father's arm with one hand, and covering her mouth with the other hand, Rika tittered.

"You guys shouldering the same shrine?"

"Probably," Rika said.

"You got your headband?"

Uruo pulled out the yellow headband out of his coat pocket and squeezed it right back into the pocket. He combed up with his fingers a wild mop of curly black hair.

"He looks great in the festival outfit, doesn't he? He should put it on every day at work." Rika's glance caressed Uruo's white boxer shorts. "Tourists would love it."

"I like my green overalls."

With her eyes, Rika licked Uruo from the top of his head down to the tightly laced white running shoes. She blushed the moment she caught Uruo watching her. Uruo's face softened, and a thin line of his lower teeth peeked through his slightly parted lips. Rika's father caught their eye contacts again, Uruo was certain.

"Okay, guys. I'd better get busy," her father said.

"Shrine number three?"

"Yeah." Extending his arms, he brought Rika and Uruo closer together. "You wait here until the Head of the Nakamise Merchant Group finishes his speech and everybody has clapped. Then go to the first shrine parked in front of the temple's main hall. Remember, the marching chant is '*Soi-ya*.'"

"Yes, sir," Uruo said.

"I'll see you later at our stall, dad."

"Kwannon Cookies," Uruo blurted out.

"You like them little things, don't you?" Rika said.

Rika and Uruo stood at the east border of the temple precinct and listened to the Nakamise head, though Uruo could not catch what he was saying. Perhaps he was too close to the microphone. Uruo kept staring at Rika's profile, which had no resemblance to Yuri's.

The smoke from the roofed incense burner in the middle of the precinct filled the air. Occasionally the breeze scattered the dense suspension of the smoke into small whirls. Rika kept fanning the smoke away from her face with her hand. Uruo drew in this aroma characteristic of Buddhist cemeteries. Millions of tiny stars ignited behind his eyes and blinded him momentarily. Pepper pricked everywhere in his brain. When his vision returned, he recognized Ibe sitting on stage in the parapet of the temple as one of the four Nakamise representatives behind the Head now speaking.

Greeted by carriers her own age, Rika led the way to the parked portable shrine. She positioned herself at the rightmost vertical pole, between the portable shrine and the gold-plated end piece of the pole. Uruo intended to slip behind Rika.

"Yo! You—" Pointing his finger at Uruo, the chief attendant stopped him and stared at Uruo's dark bewildered face. The attendant's gaze halted at Uruo's coat lapels that read "Ibe Tempura."

"I apologize," the attendant said, bowing deep. The lower half of his face smiled, but his eyes below the furrowed brow disbelieved what he was witnessing. "I had no idea you were with Mr. Ibe."

"Not a problem," Uruo said, nonchalant.

"Please take your position behind this Kwannon Cookies lady."

"'Cookie lady?' Is that you?" Uruo chuckled.

"I'm glad something is funny." Rika pushed Uruo away.

Still laughing, Uruo took a position behind her, then crouched down to shoulder the pole. And, following most carriers of the shrine, he put his right hand on Rika's right shoulder. Rika took his hand and placed it around her waist.

All the carriers rose, their arms wrapped around the poles that secured the portable shrine.

"*Soi-ya!*" the principal carrier shouted.

"*Soi-ya*!" all other carriers responded.

With the carriers' bouncy small steps going forward, the shrine came alive, swinging up and down, left and right, riding the rhythm of the shout. The shrine made a 180-degree turn toward Kaminari Gate, to exit the temple precinct to parade in the streets of Asakusa.

Ten minutes into the parade, Uruo became aware of a hand placed on his right shoulder. The hand belonged to a carrier behind Uruo, who was perhaps one or two years older than he was. The young man's spirited shouts dominated all the rest. Uruo alternated his shout with his: one louder than the young man's, the other softer than his. The young man caught on to Uruo's vocal game and joined in. Uruo looked back at him. And they both nodded to the rhythm of the shout. Then Rika joined. The alternative shouting rippled, and all carriers got in tune with them.

At the east corner of Matsuya Department Store was a bamboo shack constructed on a truck where three children each beat drums of different sizes. All of these drums pitched high and did not echo, like tambourines without the jingling—hollow and dry. Accompanied by the drums, a flute tune traveled over the shouts. Uruo, shouting with the carrier group, listened to this old tune—delicate and forlorn. The tune seemed not to blend in with the ceaseless festive noise the street-packed spectators and shrine carriers generated. The flute tune sounded as if coming from somewhere far away, endorsing the spirit residing in the portable shrine as a bearer of good fortune. As the shrine headed south toward Sumida River, the tune and drum beat dwindled. Only the shouts filled the city.

"Pardon me, sir." An attendant stood by Uruo. "It's time to switch, sir." Uruo's replacement was standing behind the attendant.

Uruo looked at his watch. He had been shouldering the shrine for forty-five minutes. As he unwrapped his arm from the pole, dull aches from his left shoulder and upper arm collided at the joint. Rika slipped a folded paper into his palm holding Rika's waist. With a thud in his heart, Uruo tacked the paper under the waistband of his bright white boxer shorts.

Uruo left his position vacant for his replacement.

~

Two days following the festival, Uruo requested an unpaid day off from Ibe.

"The shrine was heavier than you thought, wasn't it?" Smothering a smile, Ibe gazed into Uruo's unsettling eyes for a few seconds. "Enjoy." He said nothing more.

Having lived in Asakusa for two years, Uruo knew this part of the city well, but not the whole Tokyo region. He was unsure where Shinbashi was, except that it was located somewhere south of downtown Tokyo. He stopped at the Asakusa guide building near Kaminari Gate. A male clerk with a pair of thick black-rimmed glasses gave him two options: either to take the national railway which required one transfer; or to take the subway straight to Shinbashi which would take about half an hour. Uruo chose the subway. But the idea of riding inside a tube underground sounded frightening to Uruo.

At the Asakusa subway stop, he stepped into a clean silver car with six units of long navy-blue seats and sat down near the car's middle door. Holding onto his travel bag, Uruo studied one by one the advertisement flyers framed in the space between the ceiling and the windows. Stocks, insurances, banks, department stores, college correspondence courses, among others. An ad for miso ramen caught Uruo's attention. He had tasted onion and tofu ramen, which was always plain because of the lightly seasoned chicken broth. But if miso soup replaced chicken broth, Uruo speculated, the taste would be thicker and saltier. He decided to try miso ramen for lunch that afternoon if he could.

Uruo arrived at the Shinbashi station and exited onto the east square. A police station stood in the middle of the square. Uruo's target was The Shinbashi School of Cosmetology, which was supposed to be located on the east side of Shinbashi. He went straight to the police station and asked where the cosmetology school was. The policeman folded a newspaper he was reading and came over to the entrance where Uruo was standing and asked Uruo to repeat the name of the school. Uruo pulled out a square piece of paper from his pants pocket. The police officer glanced at the name on the paper. He pointed to a wide street behind the police station that ran north and south. "This street. Two traffic lights. On the left side." He bowed to Uruo, then returned to his desk and picked up his newspaper.

The direction sounded like code to Uruo but he followed it: first passing two traffic lights, and then scrutinizing all of the signboards identifying stores and buildings. Uruo went to the end of the block that started with the second traffic light. He then retraced the same pavement. A finance company building and a bakery with coffee shop flanked the school building whose exterior cemented white stones cut in square. Above the rotating door was the name of the school carved in black relief.

Uruo pushed the rotating door. The back side of the rotating door hit his ankle. He nearly stumbled. In the lobby, he waited by a tall evergreen plant in a pot, gently tracing his fingers on a leaf to see if it was real or imitation.

A woman in a starched white lab coat opened the door by the elevator and came out to the lobby.

"Is there a student by the name of Yuri?" Uruo inquired before she greeted him.

She bowed with her gaze fixed on Uruo.

For the first time in his life, he was mesmerized how stunning a woman's facial makeup could be. Her eyebrows were drawn in a measured upward curve in dark brown; her eyelashes, also dark brown, were longer than normal and noticeably turned up; and her eyes were outlined in thick black which made them look larger than they were. Her bright red lipstick contrasted with her black hair that was cut short at her nape, permed and oiled.

"How may I help you?"

"I came to see Yuri. I understand she is a student here at the school."

"She was."

"You mean she dropped out?"

The woman tittered, then said, "She graduated this past March. And Salon Noémie hired her immediately. Are you a relative of hers?"

"We grew up together."

"At St. Veronica's?"

"Yes."

"How considerate of you to visit your sister." She pulled out her hands out of the coat pockets. "Salon Noémie is across from Théâtre Tokyo on Ginza First Street. Once you're at the movie theater, you'll have no problem finding it."

"Thank you, um …"

"It's Wada. I run the school."

"Uruo Yusa."

"Oh, Uruo. Yes. I remember Yuri often spoke of you, so fondly." Wada raised her eyebrows, cocked her head a little to left, and pursed her red lips. "Make a right at the traffic light, walk straight to Ginza Central Street, then make a left. And go all the way to First Street. It intersects with Central.

"Thank you, Miss Wada." Uruo bowed to her.

"Nice meeting you, Uruo."

Miss Wada came out to the pavement as Uruo headed for the traffic light. At the corner, Uruo looked back. They waved to each other.

~

The bench he was sitting on in the Théâtre Tokyo square squeaked.

Despite having slept with Rika the night of the festival, Uruo kept convincing himself it was Yuri he was with. While he was inside Rika, she transformed into Yuri. When they were finished and exhausted, Rika's glassy gaze kept caressing Uruo, as if she was seeking something Uruo could not give. Neither of them said anything. He put on his pants and spring jacket and left her apartment. He wanted to see Yuri badly.

Uruo leaned forward. He fixated on two women coming out of the Salon Noémie building. One of them was Yuri, he was certain. But she was no longer the Yuri whose image he had treasured since she left St. Veronica's Home. The woman he was peering at stood straight. Her breasts stood out. Her legs were long and sturdy in shining black high heels. Short blond hair accentuated her nut-brown skin. Flawless makeup, like Miss Wada's, drew everyone's attention. Her lively hand gestures and quickly changing countenance indicated pride and confidence she must have cultivated while attending the cosmetology school.

Uruo stood up, then crossed First Street in long strides. "Pardon me. You must be Yuri."

The blond woman looked back. Her eyes bulged, her mouth wide open. "I don't believe it. Uruo! My little brother, Uruo!"

They locked in hug. Yuri smelled of high society, and it sent a signal down through his thighs. He wanted keep Yuri in his embrace; he did not want to let her go; he wished they were in bed.

"Lord, what a place to bump into each other." Yuri raised her face. "You haven't changed much."

Uruo lowered his lips close to hers. She evaded him while in embrace and suggested: "Let's go to the coffee shop half a block away from here."

The other woman, slightly older than Yuri, gestured that she would go ahead on First Street without her. And Yuri consented. She did not let go of Uruo's arm: She coiled her arms around his and leaned her head on his shoulder. She remembered the day they encountered the snake on the rooftop of the incineration building. She talked about it while gazing at Uruo's profile. Beneath her thick eyelashes were a couple of gentle dark brown eyes that Uruo had never forgotten.

At the coffee shop Rio Grande, Yuri ordered a cup of whisky tea and a sandwich; Uruo ordered a cup of coffee and a plain hamburger without a bun. While eating her sandwich, one of her hands kept touching his; and, sometimes, he would hold her hand and squeeze it.

"Yuri," Uruo said suddenly. "I fell in love with you that day." It shocked Uruo how easily these words came out of his mouth when for years they had been stuck in his throat.

"I knew it," Yuri said.

"Then why didn't you say something?"

Yuri pretended to read Uruo's palm.

"Is it because you were in love with Marendo?" Uruo asked. "Did you sleep with him, Yuri?"

"I liked him a lot, just as I liked you like my little brother. Marendo is drop-dead gorgeous. When he is older, women won't leave him alone."

"What was wrong?"

Silence persisted. "I like girls, Uruo."

"Of course, you do. At the Home you were always with girls. You grew up with them."

"You don't understand … I cannot love boys."

"Why not?"

"Because—" She sipped her tea and dropped her eyes on the artificial bouquet of yellow roses in the center of their table.

Yuri's hand slipped out of Uruo's.

August 1969

ONE DAY, Uruo received a package from Marendo. The package was square and flat. It had been packed with precision, all the sides taped equally with brown packing tape, and Uruo's address written in thick-lined calligraphy. The return address indicated it had been mailed from St. Veronica's. It felt like a notebook or a magazine.

Uruo could not make sense out of Marendo sending him this package after three years of silence. According to his calculations, Marendo must have graduated from IHS in Yokohama in the past June. Uruo did not recall Marendo saying anything about his plan after high school. If he obtained a job, then he would not be at St. Veronica's; and the package would have come from somewhere else. If he were preparing to go abroad, then he might have returned to St. Veronica's briefly—and his trip should have been scheduled within a month or a month and half at the latest.

As he opened the package with a pair of small scissors used for cutting toenails, Uruo was thinking about Marendo. Why the three years of silence? It had created a distance between them. But then it occurred to him that, when he left Chinosaki, he had told Marendo he wanted to live his new life in the way he deemed fit. It was possible, Uruo surmised, that Marendo let Uruo alone by keeping silent so that Uruo could focus on advancing forward with his life. But he was curious that the desire to resume his friendship with Marendo was absent in him. Three years was a long time too.

The package contained a copy of *Daily Shōnan* dated Tuesday, August 4, 1970. Marendo had folded the newspaper in a way that Uruo could at once locate the article in question. Marendo had also marked with a red arrow where the article started.

"Inga's murdered?" Uruo whispered to himself.

The newspaper article reported that her dead body had been found in a ditch near Yokosuka Playhouse. It had been floating in the ditch for a few days before being discovered by a theater patron. This woman said she could not tell what was stuck in the ditch at first. She thought it looked like a "greasy clod," she said. Then she noticed something that looked like seaweeds: It was hair. She called the police from the public phone in the theater. By the time this patron came out of the theater, a crowd of onlookers packed the road above the ditch. Three policemen arrived. They pulled the dead body out of the ditch, slipped it into a plastic bag and zipped it up, and then put the bag in the black minivan waiting behind the police car. The coroner's office found out that the dead person was a black female—of mixed race, about seventeen or eighteen years old. She had a trace of a vertical cut on her left cheek.

The report continued: There was an anonymous call from a woman. She reported that she had seen a young black girl with heavy makeup, wearing a tight blouse and a miniskirt, visit a Singaporean student's lodging. This anonymous call came from the Singaporean's neighbor.

The word "abnormal" appeared in the article four times. And it bothered Uruo. According to the article, Inga had got into perverse lovemaking after she became acquainted with a Singaporean student named Dasha Halim who lived two blocks from her house. Her death was accidental, the article said. During their lovemaking—which turned out to be their last—Halim throttled her with his necktie to intensify her pleasure. He had gone overboard with it and choked her to death. Halim had thrown her body in the ditch. The police caught him at Haneda International Airport. Inga was twenty years old.

Toward the end, the article quoted Sister Ōgin—that Inga's mother took custody of her when she turned fifteen. This was her only remark. Then it mentioned that Father Sainen, the deputy executive director of St. Veronica's Home, had taken the responsibility of communicating with the media. One line in the article captured Uruo's attention: "When Inga came to us, she already had the scar on her left cheek."

"No, she didn't!"

Uruo read the line again. These words were Father Sainen's. The newspaper quoted his lie. Would he go into hiding like he had done after he tied Marendo and Uruo to the tree before Sister Ōgin flogged them? Sainen was trying to protect someone, or something, with his lie—the children at St. Veronica's? Sister Ōgin and her family honor? Or both? Suddenly a grotesque speculation pierced his heart: Sainen lied to the media because he was afraid of Sister Ōgin's retaliation.

Like the cracked branch of the camphor tree that almost killed him, Uruo's faith in Father Sainen had cracked long before when Yuri told him Sainen had tied Marendo and him to the tree. Now, it had suddenly snapped in two, pulled down by the weight of this gross lie.

A supposed man of Christ, a friend of the children, and a protector of those whom Sister Ōgin prosecuted. But above all that, Sainen was a skilled administrator. He made certain that the children were fed, that they were taught well at school, and that they were provided a family-like atmosphere. His consideration gave rise to his "small-cluster" concept—a scheme which assigned fourteen children to a house mother in a dormitory. A man of such attributes. A man who was loved and revered by all. Yet this man denied the truth. Then Uruo heard another voice trembling in his heart: What would have happened if Father Sainen had told the truth? Uruo's chest tightened. A deep sigh quivered out through his lips. The police would arrest Sister Ōgin, St. Veronica would close its gates, and the children would have nowhere to go. Sister Ōgin had to be protected in order to save the children—was this what happened? Was it his intent? If the media uncovered that Sister Ōgin had cut into Inga's face with a saw, what would happen? Wouldn't the media demand a justification for the public statement Sainen had made? What an audacious misrepresentation of the incident. A person who could falsify a fact for a certain higher purpose must be fearless, self-assured, and ruthless.

No longer could Uruo sustain his faith in Sainen's caregiving, his disapproval of Sainen's lie, and his condemnation of Sainen's fraudulence. It all plummeted. Not because Uruo sanctioned the way Sainen handled the media, but because the interdependence of right and wrong in real life presented itself as something far beyond the Bible studies and church practices that he had trained as a believer of Christ.

This disparity alarmed Uruo, turning him inward. Sainen was not the only hypocrite. Wouldn't Uruo, too, be a hypocrite to disregard his spirituality during the three years since he left St. Veronica's? No Bible, no church, no hymns. Why? Was he avoiding it all on purpose? Uruo wanted to think he left the past all behind so that he could focus on what awaited before him, not what had gone on behind him. Uruo wanted to grow up to be a man who could embrace all that he was born with. He wanted to be a man who could embrace whatever confronted him. He didn't want to look back.

Uruo stretched on the *tatami* floor and rested his head on his folded arms. He wanted his mind to go blank. He wanted it to slip into a trance where no thoughts would cross one another. The harder he tried to enter this trance, the louder the noise from Nakamise Street amplified. Never had he been so aware of how clamorous the city was. He had lived in it for three years.

His fondness for soundless ambience was a new discovery for him. It caught him off guard. In Mitsukaidō, Nao, Cousin Hanbo, and neighborhood friends doted on him. In Chinosaki, brothers and sisters of his kind surrounded him day and night, in school and in his dormitory. And in Asakusa, the ceaseless city clamor and the visitors never left him. He thought nothing of these living noises around him. Now his heart traveled back to Mitsukaidō—to the forest behind the train station where the Jizō statue with its little red napkin stood alone.

The forest veiled itself in deep green. The cryptomeria, the pines, the chinquapins, all soaring into the sky, made the forest look like a black mountain—reticent and watchful. The murmur of leaves touched him with faint aloofness. The forest remained silent. Uruo pretended he was lying on his back on a quilt of dead leaves. Here, in the forest, he was certain, he could clear his mind for hours. The forest was the stillness he craved.

January 1970

FROM THE kitchen phone in the stall Uruo dialed Ibe's living room number. Ibe picked up the receiver.

"Have you thought about my proposal, sir?" Uruo made himself sound assertive.

"Yes, I have."

"And?"

"It took a while—to be honest with you. As you know, I wanted to keep my business within a controllable range."

"I understand, sir."

"But my final decision is yes, under one condition—that you take full responsibility for what you came up with. It's not a small change that we anticipate. It's a major one."

"I very much appreciate your trust."

"Make sure to add five percent delivery fee on each group order."

"I will start delivery only for orders greater than seven people as a group. The payment will be cash only, no charge accounts—at least for the first six months."

"Good. Start managing your own delivery unit. It's all yours. Let me see what you can do."

"I am grateful, sir." Uruo put down the receiver and jumped for joy.

On the other hand, when the initial excitement subsided, Uruo was peeved as to why it had taken Ibe two months to arrive at his final decision. Uruo at once recalled how long it had taken for Ibe to issue affirmative permission to put *Uruo fusion* both on the paper menu and on the wall menu: Two years. This menu proposal, Uruo was certain, offended Ibe—in Ibe's view there was no business the fifteen-year-old black indentured apprentice had in telling him, or even advising him, that the practices of his family business needed upgrading for today's market. While Ibe kept complaining about so many changes occurring around him, the rate and amount of profit that *Uruo fusion* tempura had brought in had fattened up Ibe's wallet. Only then Ibe saw the commercial value of Uruo's creation and was convinced, at last, to publicize the *fusion* on the menu.

As for Uruo's delivery proposal, Ibe had deliberated for two months. Knowing Ibe for three years now, Uruo had learnt how Ibe viewed and thought out things around him: Through his loyalty to his ancestors. It had taken time, but Uruo apprehended how deeply rooted Ibe's ancestorial loyalty was—it was the center of Ibe's thinking and his decision-making processes. Such an old-fashioned way of thinking had, often, hindered Uruo's eagerness to adopt current trends in marketing—it hindered Uruo like a stone wall. For Uruo, business meant money making. For Ibe, it meant honoring his ancestors and his family legacy. He could not continue swimming against the current; otherwise, his tempura business would collapse—Uruo reflected. Maybe Ibe had always been aware of it. Uruo supposed it on the basis of Ibe's recent mentioning of his retirement and of his "old age"—he was perhaps in his mid-sixties, Uruo had guessed. Uruo recognized a golden dot shining on the horizon to which his path connected. Uruo was determined to march straight to that shiny golden dot.

The first request for delivery order came a week after Uruo had contacted the telephone book publisher and the Asakusa Information Center. With Ibe's permission, he also added to the Ibe Tempura signboard the notice "We deliver," with the store phone number below it.

This order—a total of twenty-four dishes, each dish with three pieces of fusion tempura—came from Takara Hotel located along Sumida River where a fund-raising banquet was held for the Tange Scholarship Foundation. Uruo recognized the name "Tange," but dismissed it as a coincidence. Surely other people in Japan had that name.

At seven o'clock in the evening, Uruo arranged his fusion tempura in dishes made of bamboo-shoot skins, laying six of each into four flat wooden boxes that could stack up and lock on top of one another. He tied them with ropes and attached them to the back seat of his bicycle. He was already dreaming of getting his driver's license so that Ibe might agree to the purchase of a small truck for delivery, which would expand his delivery radius and, subsequently, increase his profits.

Uruo parked his bicycle at the back entrance of the Takara Hotel kitchen. He carried all the pile of boxes to the kitchen where he was greeted by a catering manager, who instructed Uruo to place the pile on a spotless stainless steel cooking table. Looking at the table, Uruo immediately planned to tell Ibe about the benefits of having stainless steel counter tops in place of their old wooden counter. One major point he would make in his talk with Ibe would be a health issue—stainless steel would not allow germs to seep into the grains and cracks of the wooden counter and was easily cleaned up with a modern disinfectant. He was sure Ibe would resist at first, but Uruo was convinced he could entice Ibe with the promise of more business from an increasingly health-savvy clientele.

Uruo handed the manager an emblemed envelope with an invoice in it. The manager ushered Uruo into his office where there was a tinted one-sided window. People in the banquet room could not see the manager, but the manager could see what was going on in the banquet room. The manager signed the acknowledgement of receipt that Uruo submitted. Then Uruo signed below the manager's signature. The manager put bills in a hotel envelope, tacked the envelope's seal flap into its pocket, and, holding the envelope with both of his hands, tendered it to Uruo. The envelope felt thick in Uruo's hand. He bowed twice and put it in his small black shoulder bag. He bowed once more.

"The guests are in the Green Room for cocktail at this time. Could you please take the tempura pile to the buffet table and arrange the tempura in the middle space on the table?" The manager gave him a pair of rubber gloves and opened the door and held it for Uruo to enter the Sumida Room where the guests would dine buffet style after their cocktail.

Uruo was removing tempura from the third wooden container on to the table when he recognized a young man in tuxedo leaning against the edge of the folded room partition panels and conversing with an elderly gentleman in a black three-piece suit. The young man wore an eye patch over his left eye. His profile with a high cheek bone stirred Uruo's memory. But his memory retrieved no one in particular. The elderly gentleman shifted his position, putting his weight on his right leg. His gaze seemed to target Uruo's dark face—though Uruo could not see his face well from where he was. The young man turned halfway toward the Sumida Room. Now Uruo was the object of their scrutiny. They continued their conversation in whisper. When Uruo was about to finish arranging his bamboo-skin covered tempura, the young man—with his hands in his pants pockets—approached Uruo and stopped at a few yards away from him. The right corner of his upper lip rose, and his right eye slanted up at the corner.

Uruo stood straight, the now-emptied fourth box hanging from his hand.

"How could I ever forget you, Coal Boy."

Uruo glared at the young man. "Jōji Tange."

Jōji removed the eye patch from his left eye, deliberately. "Don't tell me you've forgotten this, Uruo." Jōji's left eye shone with strange lacquer-like luster. It did not blink, it did not move, it stared at no one.

"The black *kappa* born illegitimately of an only-*san*."

Uruo stepped back; Jōji stepped forward and continued: "The lowest scum of the earth—a reminder of defeat, a token of black-blood invasion, a dissonant voice of outsider not belonging to the lineage of our Emperor." Jōji covered his left eye with the patch. "Look at you now. A delivery servant, a slave—that's what you are. You'll never amount to anything for the rest of your life."

"You instigated that incident, Jōji. Remember?" Uruo's voice had a deep vibrato. "By the way, you don't tell me what I am, what I should do, and how I should live. I don't hide behind the riches that my parents amassed. I wasn't born with a silver spoon in my mouth—like you were, Jōji."

With their cocktail glasses, some guests began flowing into the Sumida Room for their buffet. The elderly gentleman came in and held Jōji's arm and took him back into the Green Room.

Uruo stood there until Jōji vanished into the crowd of guests.

"All is well, Mr. Yusa?"

Uruo thanked the manager for his business, his gaze still fixed on the space above the guests' incessant movements in the Green Room. Uruo then picked up the empty wooden boxes. Leaving the manager's bewildered face behind, Uruo left the hotel.

November 1970

A SHADOW SWAYED at the entrance of Uruo's lodging.

Uruo had locked the shop's back door and turned around to face the house. Ibe's living room was lit dark orange as if a candle burning. Ibe was not in.

The shadow looked up; the glass doors emitted dark silver reflections. The shadow then tilted its head to the side wall of the house. It must have heard the meowing of the cat that lived somewhere in the next block.

Uruo was not sure if this cat had an owner or if it was a stray. He had stroked its small forehead and scratched its chin before. The cat always turned over and showed her black-and-white belly, purring.

The shadow crouched and extended its hand. The cat sniffed the hand, looked up into the shadow's face, and dashed back into the bush by the house. The shadow stood up and swayed again.

"Rika?" Uruo whispered.

"It's been a while, hasn't it?"

"You disappeared, Rika ..."

Neither spoke.

"Let's go upstairs." Uruo opened the entrance door.

Rika climbed the stairs, ignoring Uruo following her.

On the second-floor foyer, Uruo passed her and turned right on the corridor and opened the sliding *shōji* screen of his room.

Rika had stayed in the foyer, silent.

"C'mon in." He closed the *shōji* screen after her.

Rika approached the folding table, put her brown purse with a thin shoulder strip on it, looked straight at the glass doors on the west side of his room, still not a word.

Uruo followed her.

Rika stood motionless, her back to him.

Uruo stopped.

Rika turned around.

Stunned at Rika's bulging eyes, Uruo stepped back.

Rika's right hand smacked Uruo's left cheek.

Uruo's head flipped right.

She slapped his right cheek.

Numbed, Uruo stared at her.

"You got me pregnant!" Another right-hand blow landed on his left cheek.

"I had a baby boy. Black as coal, just like his father!"

"No!" Uruo's hands locked Rika's neck, throttling her. If he wanted to choke her at that moment because she had given birth to his child, or because he resented that the baby was black like him, he could not decide—he just wanted her gone.

Veins stressed her temples and forehead.

Shocked at himself, Uruo let go of his hands, stared at them as if they belonged to somebody else. No words traversed his brain, but an image of Inga strangulated by a Singaporean.

Her hands charged at his throat. He grabbed her arms, rendering her immobile. But she escaped his grip. Rika attempted to beat her fists on his chest. Uruo clutched her wrists. Foam leaked out of the corners of her lips.

"Cool it, woman!" He threw her against the *tatami* floor.

A convulsion drove a volcanic wailing out of her gut. It disgorged all that she had kept bottled up inside.

Uruo stepped back, anticipating her renewed assault.

Her wailing ebbed away. She raised her upper body. Half of her eyeballs sucked under her upper eyelids, turning white. Uruo stepped back.

"I hate you, Uruo Yusa." Her jaw joints spasmed. "You tainted me with your black blood. I'll never forgive you for that."

She snatched her purse and stood up straight.

Uruo backed away once again and grabbed the pole at the alcove behind. He was sure her purse was about to strike his head.

Rika glared at him.

Uruo stepped forward, stopped, then once again forward.

Rika remained still.

With his eyes Uruo traced the outline of her angular face and then touched her shoulders.

She let his hands stay on her.

Invisible quivers seeped into Uruo's hands from her shoulders. The remnant of her wailing, now hardly audible, pushed her chest in and out like the bellows of a church organ. She slowly embraced Uruo's chest and, burying her face in the base of his thick beck, let it all out.

Uruo held her tight; she returned his feverish embrace. Slowly, Uruo made a gentle move down toward the *tatami* floor, which Rika followed without resistance. They sat leaning against the table, still in embrace.

"Where is the baby?" Uruo whispered to Rika's ear.

"I don't know. A dark-skinned couple was waiting outside the labor room at the hospital to become my baby's new parents."

"You left Nakamise because you knew you were pregnant?"

"No. I wanted to get away from my parents and hometown. I found out about my pregnancy much later. I was staying with my older sister then. She first saw the signs. I didn't know anything about having children."

"I will never see my boy, then."

"No. I won't either. I signed him away, for his own good."

"Why did you come back?"

"I wanted to tell you about your baby. I wanted to see my baby's father one more time, Uruo."

"You don't hate me because I loved you?"

"How can I?" Rika raised her upper body and repositioned herself so that her legs were resting side way. Her back leaned against his chest and her fingers braided with his stubby fingers. "I'm sorry for that crazy tantrum—I just had to let it all out. You were the only person I could do that to. They say you get mad at the person you love most."

He held her tighter and nestled his cheek against hers.

"Are you staying here?"

"No. I must go back to Shikoku Island tonight. By express."

"You have a man waiting for you there?"

Looking at his fingers intertwined with hers, she murmured: "I won't let you know one way or the other."

"Why not?" Uruo brought his lips near hers.

She evaded him by a slight move of her face.

When Uruo returned from Ueno Station after he had seen Rika off that night, his chest blazed with guilt that refused to define itself. A black baby boy, who came into this world only to be given away. Rika's earnest confession did not convince Uruo that he had fathered her child. Even the words Rika had spit out at him in rage—so real, so compelling—could not. Those words could have been part of a stage play she might have written. And then she had given a virtuoso performance of it, playing the principal actor, with Uruo as her supporting cast. It was a possibility that Rika could have slept with other black men in Tokyo and one of them had fathered the child. Uruo had never seen this baby boy, nor had he ever held him in his arms. How could he know any of this was true?

Her return to Asakusa was unfathomable to him. It could be that she wanted him to know he was involved in the birth of her baby. More palpable yet, she had gone mad and she had no knowledge of it. No matter the circumstance, the probability of his fathering of Rika's black baby loomed ominous. It frightened him.

He could continue forward with his life as if nothing had happened—just like Rika would have in Shikoku. But the voice, like a swishing in distance, haunted Uruo: "Didn't you impregnate her with that child?" He did not deny this voice, try as he might. But then it was Rika who had wanted Uruo, and she wanted it more than once. He had given her what he thought she wanted, because he wanted to please her, because he wanted her to love him. Was this merely a thought of a naïve eighteen-year-old boy who failed to link the passion of consensual lovemaking to possible parenthood? He could not pinpoint where his fright was coming from. Not from the baby boy. Nor from Rika.

Simply fathering a child would be distinct from being a father to that child. Only a man worthy of fatherhood could dissolve this distinction. If Uruo had indeed fathered Rika's child, could he have ever been a true father to the child? Uruo shuddered at the thought that he could have become the man who had fathered him after loving his mother and left them all behind.

Uruo had only vague memories of the man he used to call "Dad," a man who was one day simply no longer there, leaving behind an emptiness that his family could only fill in part. The thought that he had now fathered a son who would never even know him as his own "Dad" made Uruo feel hollow and afraid.

May 1971

DRESSED IN a dark gray suit accentuated by a high-collared, button-down white shirt with a light gray necktie, Uruo entered the reception room of St. Veronica's Home for the first time in four years. Perhaps because had Uruo grown larger, the room gave the impression that it had shrunk on its own. The décor of the room remained the same: The table and the chairs on which Sister Ōgin, Father Sainen, Nao, and Uruo himself had sat so many years ago looked unchanged. The furniture seemed to have grown darker with more and more polish seeping into the grains, covering up years of flaws and small scratches. A semicircular brick-colored leather couch was the only thing that was new. For the first time, Uruo noticed how the floor-to-ceiling bookcase housed all hardcover books, mostly in English.

Uruo approached the right wall where Sister Ōgin's portrait hung. It was a charcoal drawing. Inscrutability oozed out of the portrait—brilliant and aloof.

"Welcome, Uruo Yusa!" Father Sainen came in wearing his cassock. He held Uruo's arms in his hands and said, "Ibe has nothing but praise for you. He thinks you are already a far-sighted and able businessman."

"Thank you, Mr. Sainen. Mr. Ibe is a good man." Uruo maintained his composure—respectful but distant.

"Let's sit there in the couch." Sainen's mass of black hair had grown into a tuft of pure silver. The purple wart on the left side of his nose seemed to have grown larger, like a gnarl on a tree. He took a pair of spectacles from his cassock pocket and hooked them onto his nose. He then sat down on the couch at the opposite side of where Uruo sat. Through his spectacles, Sainen scrutinized Uruo whose gaze rested on Sainen's wrinkleless forehead.

"It is rather curious that you now call me 'Mr. Sainen.' It leads me to presume that something has caused an important change in you. Or perhaps you have outgrown the kind of life you were taught to live while you were growing up here at St. Veronica's." Sainen's voice lacked the confidence and dominance of the father figure Uruo had remembered, a man who had raised displaced racially mixed children like Uruo, whom the media called "the excreta of the war." Uruo did not blink. Sainen continued: "May we start our conversation by discussing what caused the change in you, and how it has affected you that you have the need to address me as 'Mr.'?"

"Yes, sir." Uruo's hazel eyes shone with strange aggression, the strength of rebellion. "I wanted to see you because only you can answer some questions that have stayed with me for all these years." Uruo turned to Sister Ōgin's portrait hung on the wall. "When the weather is cold, my back throbs with pain. You remember what Ōgin did to me, I'm sure."

"I remember that *Sister* Ōgin could become zealous in her official duties, yes," Sainen said, sighing. "Do you really have such little regard for your caretakers, my son?"

"Please call me 'Yusa.'"

"Well, then, Yusa, what is it you are trying to convey?"

"That day, Marendo and I were tied to the tree and whipped and whipped and whipped. Marendo fell unconscious." Uruo tightened his lips. "It's confused me to this day why you tied us to the tree and let her punish us, and then you just disappeared."

"You are accusing me of the participation in child abuse."

"Yes. You not only knew about it, but you helped that monster."

"Monster! What makes you assert yourself this way, Yusa?"

"The truth. When you were preparing me and Marendo for the punishment, Inga saw it all from the girls' washroom."

"Was she positive it was I who was an accomplice to the punishment?"

Uruo's aggressive glare gripped Sainen, Uruo pointed to the left slope of his nose with his index finger. "You had a hooded black jacket on, but she saw your face clearly in the morning sunlight. She had no doubt it was you."

Sainen averted his gaze onto the old table that he had known since the founding of St. Veronica's. "Can she attest to it now?"

"Inga is dead, Mr. Sainen—and you know it." Uruo paused. "But many of us kids heard it from Inga. She never lied: She couldn't—that was her nature. I want you to admit that you tied us to the tree, Mr. Sainen."

"No, I did not." Sainen swallowed deep while he kept his gaze on the table. His right hand dug into the side of the couch.

"Then who did Inga see in the hooded black jacket?"

"I'm afraid I have no knowledge of the person who helped tie you boys to the tree."

Uruo stared at Sainen's profile, detecting almost invisible twitches at the corner of Sainen's mouth. "Inga was telling the truth."

"Why don't you trust me any longer, son?"

"*Yusa*, please."

"Why, then, Yusa?"

"In the *Daily Shōnan* article about Inga last August, Mr. Sainen, you said that when Inga came to St. Veronica's she already had the scar on her left cheek."

"Where did you see that article? The newspaper does not circulate in Tokyo. Did anyone send it to you?"

"That's not the issue. It's that you ..." Uruo's throat trembled as he sucked in the air. "You lied. For all of these years, you've been lying to us."

Sainen stood up, his hands in his cassock pockets. He walked over to the large window and turned slightly to where he could see the holly bush and the pebbled path. "It sounds cruel—the term 'lie.' Unfortunately, sometimes life requires us all to confront circumstances in which we have no choice but to alter the facts in question."

"And Inga's murder forced you to cover it up."

"Not a 'cover up.' An 'adjustment of facts,' Yusa."

"To protect Ōgin's family honor and her own reputation? Shouldn't her child abuse—her illness be reported?"

"I'm sure she would be exposed if the board members were to approve of it. But they have not done so, and they will not do so. My decisions must always align with the board members' intentions."

"If you get to change facts, then how can you preach honesty and love for your neighbor? You are supposed to be a shepherd, but you lead your sheep to the slaughter!"

"I am a human, Yusa, not a saint. Neither are you. Our action stems from our instinct to survive. I am a priest by profession, and what I say in chapel is what the profession requires."

"Then your Christian teaching must also be what your profession requires. For years we listened to you tell us about love and compassion. But …" Uruo's voice flattened but pointed. "But your teaching has been all just words. Empty words."

"Yusa, I think you are forgetting one important fact: That you are still under Ibe's guardianship. Until the Coming-of-Age Day when you are twenty years old."

"Is that a threat, Mr. Sainen? Yes, I will be twenty years old next January. Even if you are planning to ship me off to a reform school and keep me behind bars, I'll be out in just a few months. And don't forget that I have the newspaper article with your statement about what happened to Inga. Inga was wounded during her stay at St. Veronica's, not before. Many people could attest to that. And you will have to answer to the media, Mr. Sainen. It could be the end of your career."

"Oh," Sainen said, sighing. "Where has my son gone?"

"He has grown up. He is about to become a legal adult. And he will need no guardians who 'adjust facts' for him."

"Why do we have to part like this?" Sainen leaned against the windowsill and held his arms around his chest.

"You were Ōgin's right hand in torturing me and Marendo. You lied to protect Ōgin. For the rest of my life, Mr. Sainen, the whip scar across my back will remind me that you're not a shepherd protecting his sheep, but a wolf hidden under that cassock."

Sainen's lip quivered. He uttered no words.

Uruo stood up and buttoned his suit.

January 1972

THE 1972 Coming-of-Age Day fell on Saturday, January the fifteenth. Uruo had turned twenty on January the fifth, but he had to wait until January the fifteenth to officially become a legal adult. Everyone who turned twenty years of age celebrated their entry into the adult world with their families. Their citizenship rights were officially bestowed upon them, and they were treated with respect as new members of society.

Uruo did not give much thought to it. The distinction between who was a kid and who was a grownup seemed meaningless to him. Because a person, even an eighty-year-old, could be both a child and an adult at heart. This conviction came from his own formative years under the care of his grandmother and kindly friends like Mr. Gen. But Coming-of-Age Day was a tradition, just like New Year's Day, that everyone observed. Ibe was no exception.

As a congratulatory token to Uruo's official commencement into adulthood, Ibe gave him two weeks of paid vacation days. Ibe had an additional gift for Uruo that morning: Bankbooks that registered all of Uruo's savings entries for the past five years since he had become Ibe's apprentice.

"You can buy a house with your savings," Ibe joked as he handed Uruo the bankbooks in a celebratory envelope that bore an already tied double-ribbon: one red, and the other white.

"Might I buy your business with it, Mr. Ibe?"

"I like that idea. I like it a lot." Ibe patted Uruo's shoulder. "Well, when I retire, one day. How does that sound?"

"I will remind you when the time is ripe. Is that a deal?"

"Absolutely."

Uruo put the gift in his jacket's inside pocket, looking forward to opening it on the way to Mitsukaidō.

The bus timetable indicated it would take fifty minutes longer than train from Asakusa to Mitsukaidō. Uruo did not mind taking the bus because he knew it would be less crowded and he could watch the landscapes transform like a chameleon. Uruo got on a southbound bus to Mitsukaidō departing early afternoon.

After he settled into his seat and the bus started puttering out of the station, Uruo pulled out the celebratory envelope from his jacket and untied the red and white ribbons. Inside the envelope were two bankbooks and a piece of quality paper folded in four to fit the envelope. He first opened one of the bankbooks: The handwritten dates and deposit amounts in black ink aligned each page from top to bottom. The handwriting, its angular strokes, hinted at that Ibe had gone to the same bank clerk to deposit Uruo's earnings on the last day of every month. Uruo gazed at the handwriting as if it were an exhibited calligraphic scroll—admiring the bank clerk's impeccable hand movement, impressed by the beauty of each letter and number. Then he opened the folded paper which bore a simple heading: List of Deductions. Uruo stared at the heading—in the past five years Ibe had not once mentioned or discussed any such deductions. Uruo's lodging and food were supposed to be all free, in exchange for services that included cleaning Ibe's house and operating his tempura stall every day. The list recorded five main entries summarizing his rent and breakfast of every month for each of his five years with Ibe, to the end of last December the thirty-first. The grand total of the deductions came to about one-third of Uruo's entire earnings for all five years. His net gain was not small, but it could have been much larger—it could have been large enough to set up a seed money account for him to start his own tempura shop in the future. He would have to work two more years to regain the whole amount, he calculated. Sainen had never told him that this financial arrangement would come with Ibe's guardianship. Whether Ibe had imposed deductions on Uruo's earnings from the beginning, or if Sainen had suggested that Ibe make the deductions, Uruo could not pinpoint. He folded the deduction list and put it back in the envelope.

His forehead churned hot and his vision turned blurry. He did not doubt that he had been cheated, been taken advantage of. Anger burnt Uruo. In the midst of his furry, Uruo at once determined that he would increase the frequency of his daily delivery trip and would raise the price per delivery slightly—these increases would compensate all the deductions that had been taken away from him. And people like Tange family could easily afford the costs. Why shouldn't they pay more?

Uruo foresaw that, in several months, his delivery system would overpower Ibe's old-fashioned way of selling tempura at the stall—particularly in terms of profits. And he would be the one to control the money. He would be the one to take his daily earnings to the bank: He would close his current bank account which Ibe could access and open his own account that only he himself could manage. Uruo now saw it crystal clear why Marendo stayed away from grownups. They were chameleons: Their colors changed depending on whom they were with, where they were, what they were doing—and these conditions determined how they ought to fabricate appropriate appearances to be seen and accepted. Grownups excelled in playing this game, and children were often the losers.

If Sainen and Ibe played this same game, then how would Cousin Hanbo, Chisa, and Nao act towards Uruo?

It had been seven years since Uruo hugged Nao. And it had been fourteen long years since the day he waved to Hanbo from the departing steam engine at the Mitsukaidō station, yelling at Hanbo that he would come home that evening. A long separation and then reunion … Uruo should have been jumping up and down with joy, but his trepidation dissuaded him from doing so. He wanted his family to be no different from how they had remained in his memory. What if they were like strangers? What if the long distance had separated them to the point of no return? Uruo had changed—he was no longer the boy they had held, loved, and protected, which meant they too must have changed. Maybe Nao and Cousin Hanbo were thinking the same thing—would Uruo be the boy they once knew? And they too might be afraid to face Uruo now.

After three hours of the bus ride, the vehicle parked in a small outdoor bus terminal by the Mitsukaidō train station. Only one other passenger got off. The cold air pricked Uruo's ears. He put his *ushanka* hat on. He had fished this hat out of a pile of Salvation Army clothes that arrived from America while he was still in St. Veronica's. They were piled up high in the chapel's all-purpose room, waiting to be sorted out. Uruo was a sixth grader, he recalled. Back then the hat was too loose. Now it was tight about his forehead: the abundance of his curly hair made it smaller. He turned up his coat collar and secured it with his scarf and then shouldered his rucksack.

The bus made a sharp turn and headed east.

Uruo dropped in at a small food market across the bus terminal. The market displayed a signboard outside that read "iron-oven roasted sweet potatoes." He ordered eight of them. A store clerk hooked one roasted potato at a time on a long stick with a bent claw attached to the tip of it and brought it up from the barrel-shaped iron-oven. He put the potato in a bag repurposed from newspaper. He repeated the hooking and bagging eight times. He then collected eight individually bagged potatoes into a corrugated cardboard box. Uruo paid for the potatoes, then squeezed the cardboard box into his rucksack, and tossed the sack on his back. Warmth from the sack seeped through and penetrated his back into his chest. The snug sensation felt heartwarming.

Namiki Street, now paved in coal-black asphalt, hinted at this old town slowly awakening to whisper of modernization. The signboard NAMIKI PHARMACY had replaced GEN'S BAKERY. Uruo stopped at the pharmacy and peeked inside through the window. Shelf after shelf of medicine bottles of all shapes and colors—it was a world unknown to him. Uruo half-expected Gen to come out of the door, with his stained apron and that sweet smell of bread. "Now my little nephew," Gen would say to him with a gentle smile and hand him a brown bag of *anpan* and watch him eat. He would then ruffle Uruo's curly mop of hair and return to his kitchen in the back, satisfied.

Across the pharmacy, where an aged pine tree used to spread its sturdy branches in all directions, stood a concrete building with four floors. There was nothing to indicate what this building was. Uruo studied it from ground up and back down. A faceless white square mass—he could make nothing else of it. He turned left at the pharmacy and headed south on Namiki Street.

A man in a pair of black corduroy and a faded windbreaker with its collar covering half of his head and face jaywalked across Namiki Street. The man's heavy boots made a quick tapping noise against the paved street.

Uruo stopped. "Hanbo?" he choked.

The man kept on walking.

"Hanbo, is that you?"

The man turned back, still walking.

"Hanbo!"

The man stood facing Uruo, frowning.

Uruo's stride quickened. "Cousin Hanbo, it's me—Uruo!"

The man blocked off the sun with his palm.

"Heavens!" Hanbo stepped forward and stopped again. His arms stretched open. "My little cousin … I can't believe it."

They embraced.

"You've come home."

Uruo nodded, his face against Hanbo's shoulder bone. A teardrop glistened in his left eye.

"Come with me," Hanbo said softly.

Uruo's chest trembled.

Inside the wooden fence of the house, Hanbo led the way to the backyard. Nao had on a winter *yukata* with splashed patterns. She was lying on a folding bamboo recliner on the veranda with all the glass doors closed—a winterized sunbathing that she loved. Her eyes were closed.

"How is she?" Uruo whispered outside the closed glass doors.

"Walking isn't that easy for her anymore. And—"

Nao's eyes opened. She stared two young men looking on to her. She frowned, opening the glass door nearest to her. "Who told you to come here, Dixon!" Nao yelled. "Aoi is dead. You should have died in Korea." She turned motionless.

Uruo froze.

"Grandma." Hanbo's serenity stunned Uruo. "This is your grandson, Uruo."

"What? Uruo? My little Uruo? Where is he?" Nao stared about, then looked up at Hanbo. "Where is Uruo?" She was appealing to him for help.

"Right here, Grandma. He's come home. Give me your hand." Hanbo took Nao's right hand and put it over Uruo's smooth walnut-colored cheek.

Nao abruptly withdrew her hand, grimaced at Uruo, then opened her eyes wide. "Oh, my grandson." She extended her arms.

Uruo hugged Nao.

Nao's tears moistened Uruo's cheek. Her warmth had a familiar scent, which took him back to those faraway days when he used to sleep between her and young Hanbo.

"Why are you two standing there? Come in. Let's sit around the foot-warmer and have some tea and cake."

"I bought some roasted sweet potatoes." Uruo pointed to the rucksack on his back.

"Sweet potatoes? Oh, you remembered those days." Nao's face wrinkled and her eyes disappeared. Uruo saw himself as a six-year-old boy.

In the kitchen foyer, Uruo flung his belted boots off and stepped into the six-*tatami* room. Chisa was standing there.

They hugged.

"Welcome home!" Chisa whispered. She took Uruo's rucksack, coat, and scarf off him. "Hm, roasted potatoes?" She took the sack into the kitchen.

As Chisa brought the potatoes and green tea to the table which housed the foot warmer, now covered with a checkered quilt, Hanbo had helped Nao into the room and seated her in a cushion. Leaving the cushion next to her for Uruo, Hanbo sat across from Nao, sticking his cold feet under the quilt.

Nao caressed Uruo's face as if he were still a baby. She said nothing. She gazed at Uruo from his massive black hair to his almond-shaped bright hazel eyes, from his thicker-than-normal lips down to his sturdy shoulder line. She nodded: "My baby."

Nao pulled the quilt up and covered her shoulders. Uruo helped her, folding the quilt across her now-hunched neck.

Chisa cut a potato in half. The potato gave off steam. She put one half of it on a small dish and put it in front of Nao.

"The potato looks good, Grandma." Uruo pointed at her potato. "So yellow. It's well roasted."

"Give him some, Chisa," Nao said.

Chisa handed Uruo a whole potato with no plate. As Uruo bit into it, she extended the potato plate to Hanbo. "Take the other half of Grandma's potato."

"Alright."

"Here, Grandma. Your green tea."

Nao bowed to the tea while chewing the potato.

"It's been a long time, Uruo," Hanbo said. "Fourteen years?"

"Yeah, since I left Mitsukaidō. Me and my buddy, Marendo, came here, though. I think it was seven years ago. But you weren't here."

"Chisa told me all about that day. I'm sorry."

"Don't be."

"By the way how is Marendo doing now?" Chisa asked.

"He went abroad two years ago."

"America?" Hanbo asked.

"No. He decided to go to Oxford. That's in England."

Hanbo nodded. "How about you, Uruo? What have you been doing?"

"I left St. Veronica's five years ago and went to Asakusa. I'm a tempura chef now. And doing great."

"So you live in Tokyo," Hanbo said, blowing on his still-steamy potato.

"You've heard of Sensō-ji Temple in Asakusa, right? My shop is right in front of it—Nakamise Street."

"It was once my dream to go to Tokyo, to work."

"I remember you used to tell me about it. It's strange I'm in Tokyo now and you stayed in Mitsukaidō."

A cheerless smile passed across Hanbo's face. "Since I got married to this lady here"—Hanbo patted Chisa's hand—"I've been running the general store with her." He paused. "It must be great to live in Tokyo."

"I don't know about that. I sometimes think of things like Mitsukaidō Pond and the forest on the other side of the train station."

"Have you thought of coming back here and open a tempura shop?"

"No. I don't think it will work, Hanbo." Uruo looked at the end piece of his potato in his hand. "I'm not wanted here. Or anywhere. I'm different. Besides, tempura businesses wouldn't do well in places like Mitsukaidō. You need a constant circulation of people."

Chisa's face brightened. "Maybe we can switch our store to a tempura eatery. And call it: Yusa's Tempura. The switch will take time, though."

"Chisa, Chisa, Chisa." Hanbo smiled and shook his head. "So creative."

"I like your idea, Chisa. I wish I can do that someday. Somewhere—I have no idea."

Chisa nodded as if she had known it was a flare-up of fancy far from reality. She poured green tea into Uruo's and Hanbo's cups.

Uruo sipped the tea and took another potato from the plate. Munching on the potato, he peeked at Nao. Her eyes were closed.

"Let her be," Hanbo whispered to Uruo. "She dozes off a lot lately."

Suddenly it dawned upon Uruo that this could be his last time with his grandmother. He touched Nao over the quilt.

Nao opened her eyes. "Yes, son?"

"Have some tea, Grandma."

"It's a delicious tea, isn't it?" She slowly reached for her teacup. "May I have some more, Kureo dear?"

Uruo's eyes widened at Chisa.

She just smiled. Leaning over the table, and holding the teapot lid with her left hand, Chisa filled Nao's teacup. All the grandchildren watched their grandmother relish the taste of her green tea. Nao put her teacup down on the table, ceremoniously.

She paused, closing her eyes for a few moments. Uruo thought to rouse her again, but then she suddenly opened her eyes and gazed into the teacup.

"I see a tea stalk, floating upright," Nao murmured. "A sign of good fortune."

The next morning, when he woke up, Uruo knew the day would be beautiful. A hole on a sliding shutter had brought the sunlight into his room. The light formed a fine beam across the room, above Uruo, and hit the wall opposite the shutters. Uruo wanted to sleep in, but his heart urged otherwise. He stacked the mattress *futon* and the cover *futon* one upon the other, then folded them in three, and pushed the pile to the corner by the bureau. When he opened the sliding shutters, the sunlight gushed into the room.

After a quick wash in the kitchen sink with freezing cold water, he was warm and fully awake. He dressed in what he had worn yesterday. Outside, he sucked in abundant mid-winter air and then, alone, headed for the terraced hill. At the hill Uruo stood by a large dark stone with small holes all over its face. He touched the stone and murmured: "How much of rain did it take to drill this many holes, I wonder." He then faced the rice paddy where he and Hanbo used to catch crayfish for dinner. He did not go there. He turned to the terraced rice paddy beyond which soared the mountain ridges. Their shape had remained the same all those years. But the swell of vibrant green that once blanketed them was not there—all leafless and gray, a color of hibernation. Even so, the radiance of the sun penetrated the gray veil over the mountains.

From the mountains, a high tide of silence surged on. Uruo watched his own breath turn into steam and evaporate. He shivered.

Acknowledgements

I am indebted to Michael Mirolla, the publisher/editor-in-chief of Guernica World Editions, who saw some literary value in my story, *Coal Boy*, and decided to publish it. When Michael contacted me regarding his decision, I was elated and frightened at the same time; so, I bombarded him with countless questions about Guernica's publication processes in minute details. Knowing that I was but an aspiring novelist, he answered every question with utmost precision and ease. In addition to his forty-four years of presence in the publishing industry, his easy and welcoming yet persistent manner impressed me greatly. The most unpublisher-like publisher/editor, with deep insight for human decency—this was my belief about Michael. Thank you, Michael, for being my publisher and editor.

Special thanks go to Michael P. Williams for his impeccable editorial work on my pre-submission manuscript of *Coal Boy*. I have known Michael for seventeen years both as a friend and as a colleague, and I have witnessed his extraordinary level of propensity toward exactitude, which he applies uncompromisingly to his problem-solving projects: a real tough professional. Without his participation, the publication of *Coal Boy* could not have materialized. Many, many thanks, Michael. You're terrific.

About the Author

A US citizen born and raised in Japan, Alban Kojima earned an M.A. in musicology from Temple University and an M.S. in information science from Drexel University in Philadelphia. For twenty-five years he held the position of Japanese Studies Informationist at the University of Pennsylvania and, at the same time, taught a graduate course entitled "Japanese Studies Resources and Problems of Research." Since late 2012, Kojima has focused on writing. He is the author of two nonfiction books published in Japanese: *Yuzo Kayama and His Music: A Global Fascination* (Tokyo: Sairyūsha, 2014); and *Alexei Sultanov* (Tokyo: Alpha Beta Books, 2017). The current work, *Coal Boy*, is his first fiction. He lives in Cherry Hill, New Jersey.